基礎文法寶典❶
Essential English Usage & Grammar

編著／J. B. Alter

審訂／劉美皇　呂香瑩

三民書局

國家圖書館出版品預行編目資料

Essential English Usage & Grammar 基礎文法寶典
／J. B. Alter編著;劉美皇,呂香瑩審訂.－－初版
二刷.－－臺北市: 三民，2019
　　冊;　　公分.－－(文法咕嚕Grammar　Guru系
列)

ISBN 978－957－14－4829－9　(平裝)

1. 英語 2. 語法

805.16　　　　　　　　　　　　　　　97018552

© **Essential English Usage & Grammar**
基礎文法寶典 1

編 著 者	J. B. Alter
審　　訂	劉美皇　呂香瑩
發 行 人	劉振強
著作財產權人	三民書局股份有限公司
發 行 所	三民書局股份有限公司
	地址　臺北市復興北路386號
	電話　(02)25006600
	郵撥帳號　0009998－5
門 市 部	(復北店) 臺北市復興北路386號
	(重南店) 臺北市重慶南路一段61號
出 版 日 期	初版一刷　2008年11月
	初版二刷　2019年1月
編　　號	S 807500

行政院新聞局登記證局版臺業字第○二○○號

有著作權・不准侵害

ISBN　978－957－14－4829－9　(平裝)

http://www.sanmin.com.tw　三民網路書店

※本書如有缺頁、破損或裝訂錯誤，請寄回本公司更換。

序

如果說，單字是英文的血肉，文法就是英文的骨架。想要打好英文基礎，兩者實應相輔相成，缺一不可。

只是，單字可以死背，文法卻不然。

學習文法，如果沒有良師諄諄善誘，沒有好書細細剖析，只落得個見樹不見林，徒然勞心費力，實在可惜。

Guru 原義指的是精通於某領域的「達人」，因此，這一套「文法 Guru」系列叢書，本著 Guru「導師」的精神，要告訴您：親愛的，我把英文文法變簡單了！

「文法 Guru」系列，適用對象廣泛，從初習英文的超級新鮮人、被文法糾纏得寢食難安的中學生，到鎮日把玩英文的專業行家，都能在這一套系列叢書中找到最適合自己的夥伴。

深願「文法 Guru」系列，能成為您最好的學習夥伴，伴您一同輕鬆悠遊英文學習的美妙世界。

有了「文法 Guru」，文法輕鬆上路！

前言

「**基礎文法寶典**」一套五冊，是專為中學生與一般社會大眾所設計，作為基礎課程教材或是課外自學之用。

英語教師往往對結構、句型、語法等為主的教學模式再熟悉不過。然而，現在學界普遍意識到**文法在語言學習的過程中亦佔有一席之地**，少了文法這一環，英語教學便顯得空洞。有鑑於此，市場上漸漸興起一股「**功能性文法**」的風潮。功能性文法旨在列舉用法並協助讀者熟悉文法專有名詞，而後者便是用以解釋及界定一語言各種功能的利器。

本套書各冊內容編排詳盡，涵蓋所有用法及文法要點；除此之外，本套書最強調的便是從不斷的練習中學好英文。每章所附的練習題皆經特別設計，提供讀者豐富多元的演練題型，舉凡**完成** (completion)、**修正** (modification)、**轉換** (conversion)、**合併** (integration)、**重述** (restatement)、**改寫** (alteration)、**變形** (transformation) 及**代換** (transposition)，應有盡有。

熟讀此書，將可幫助您完全理解各種文法及正確的表達方式，讓您在課業學習或日常生活上的英文程度突飛猛進。

給讀者的話

本書一套共五本，共分為二十一章，從最基礎的各式詞類介紹，一直到動詞的進階應用、基本書寫概念等，涵蓋所有的基本文法要義，為您建立一個完整的自修體系，並以豐富多樣的練習題為最大特色。

本書的主要細部單元包括：

USAGE PRACTICE →每個文法條目說明之下，皆有大量的例句或用法實例，讓您充分了解該文法規則之實際應用方式。

注意→很多文法規則皆有特殊的應用，或者是因應不同情境而產生相關變化，這些我們都以較小字的提示，列在本單元中。

但是我們會用→文法規則的例外情況也不少，我們在這單元直接以舉例的方式，說明這些不依循規則的情況。

小練習→每節介紹後，會有針對該節內容所設計的一段習題，可讓您即時驗證前面所學的內容。

應用練習→每章的內容結束後，我們都提供了非常充分的應用練習，而且題型豐富，各有其學習功能。建議您不要急於在短時間內將練習做完，而是漸進式地逐步完成，這樣可達成更好的學習效果。

本書文法內容完善，習題亦兼具廣度與深度，是您自修學習之最佳選擇，也可作為文法疑難的查閱參考，值得您細細研讀，慢慢體會。

基礎文法寶典 ❶
Essential English Usage & Grammar

目次

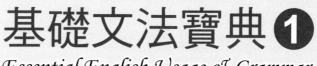

基礎文法寶典 ❶
Essential English Usage & Grammar

Chapter 1 冠 詞

1-1 不定冠詞 (a/an)

(a) 不定冠詞 a 用在以子音開頭的單數可數名詞之前。

USAGE PRACTICE

a book 一本書	a child 一個小孩	a bird 一隻鳥
a car 一輛車	a citizen 一個市民	a boy 一個男孩
a chair 一把椅子	a girl 一個女孩	a lesson 一堂課
a man 一個男人	a picnic 一頓野餐	a dog 一隻狗
a necklace 一條項鍊	a tree 一棵樹	a table 一張桌子
a hospital 一所醫院	a horse 一匹馬	a helicopter 一架直昇機
a table 一張桌子	a typewriter 一台打字機	a union 一個工會
a university 一所大學	a European 一個歐洲人	a Eurasian 一個歐亞混血兒
a 'k' 一個字母 k	a 'p' 一個字母 p	a 'c' 一個字母 c

(b) 不定冠詞 an 則用在以母音開頭的單數可數名詞之前。

USAGE PRACTICE

an egg 一個雞蛋	an axe 一把斧頭	an elephant 一隻大象
an airliner 一架客機	an umbrella 一把傘	an answer 一個答案
an American 一個美國人	an Englishman 一個英國人	an instrument 一台儀器
an arm 一隻手臂	an orange 一顆柳丁	an ice cream 一客冰淇淋
an enemy 一個敵人	an incident 一個事件	an idea 一個主意
an uncle 一位叔叔	an account 一個帳戶	an X-ray 一道 X 光線
an 'e' 一個字母 e	an 'h' 一個字母 h	an 'm' 一個字母 m
an 'o' 一個字母 o	an 's' 一個字母 s	

(c) 不定冠詞 an 也可以用在以 h 開頭但不發音的單數可數名詞之前。

an honor 一件光榮的事	**an** hour 一小時	**an** heir 一位繼承人

(d) 若名詞前有以母音開頭、或以 h 開頭但不發音的修飾詞，亦用不定冠詞 an。

USAGE PRACTICE

an old house 一間老房屋	**an** Indian man 一名印第安男子
an uneven road 一條不平坦的路	**an** unusual book 一本不平凡的書
an urban area 一個都會區	**an** honored citizen 一位榮譽市民
an oil lamp 一盞油燈	**an** honest person 一個誠實的人

但是我們會用 ➤

a happy incident 一個快樂的事件	**a** humorous story 一個幽默故事
a usual event 一個平凡的事件	**a** useful instrument 一件有用的器具
a one-dollar bill 一張一元紙鈔	**a** safety belt 一條安全帶
a one-eyed man 一個獨眼人	**a** fresh egg 一顆新鮮的蛋
a ripe orange 一顆熟了的橘子	**a** used car 一輛舊車

★若修飾詞的 **h** 有發音，或是以母音字母開頭卻仍以子音發音的情況，則還是要使用不定冠詞 **a**。

小練習

請在空格中填入不定冠詞 a 或 an。

1. _____ plant	2. _____ badminton match	3. _____ awful smell
4. _____ airy room	5. _____ university	6. _____ onion
7. _____ ripe apple	8. _____ street child	9. _____ L-shaped room
10. _____ strong objection	11. _____ European country	12. _____ able candidate
13. _____ hotel	14. _____ expensive watch	15. _____ idiom
16. _____ useful invention	17. _____ important decision	18. _____ even number
19. _____ brass urn	20. _____ home	21. _____ elbow
22. _____ early breakfast	23. _____ 'f'	24. _____ X-ray
25. _____ white elephant	26. _____ U-boat	

1-2 不定冠詞的用法

(a) 不定冠詞 a 或 an 可用來以個體代表全體。

> **USAGE PRACTICE**
>
> ▶ **A** child should obey his parents. 孩子應該服從父母。
>
> ▶ **A** cat is a lovable pet. 貓是一種可愛的寵物。

(b) 對於第一次提到的單數可數名詞，用不定冠詞 a 或 an；再次提到該名詞時，則用定冠詞 the。

> **USAGE PRACTICE**
>
> ▶ I saw **a** child. **The** child was crying. 我看見一個孩子，那孩子正在哭。
>
> ▶ **An** accident occurred at the crossroads recently. **The** accident was reported in the newspapers. 最近在這個十字路口發生一件意外，這意外被報紙報導。

(c) 不定冠詞 a 或 an 可以用在表示工作或職業的名詞之前。

> **USAGE PRACTICE**
>
> ▶ His father is **a** police officer. 他的父親是一位警官。
>
> ▶ He is **a** clerk, and his brother is **an** accountant. 他是一個店員，而他哥哥是一個會計師。
>
> ▶ She is **a** reporter at the *Daily Herald*. 她在哈洛德日報社擔任記者。

(d) 不定冠詞 a 或 an 也可以用來指某位特定人士（第一次提到的時候）。

> **USAGE PRACTICE**
>
> ▶ One afternoon, **a** beggar came to my house. 有天下午，一個乞丐到我家。
>
> （不是指任何一個乞丐，而是指特定某一個乞丐）
>
> ▶ **A** salesgirl tried to sell me some goods yesterday.
>
> 昨天有一位女售貨員試圖要賣一些商品給我。
>
> （不是任何一位女售貨員，而是指特定某一位女售貨員）

(e) 不定冠詞 a 和 an 可用在表示速度、價格、數字、時間、頻率或比率的詞語中。

> **USAGE PRACTICE**
>
> ▶ The car was going at forty kilometers **an** hour. 這輛車正以每小時四十公里的速度行駛。
>
> ▶ Eggs cost $1.20 **a** dozen. 一打雞蛋一塊兩毛美金。

▶ **An** apple a day keeps the doctor away. 一天一顆蘋果可保持健康、不用看醫生。

▶ The material costs four dollars **a** meter. 這料子一公尺四塊美金。

▶ There are ten decimeters in **a** meter. 一公尺有十公寸。

▶ The temperature is taken twice **a** day. 一天量兩次體溫。

▶ It is **a** quarter to seven now. 現在是六點四十五分。

(f) 通常人名前不加冠詞，但若不知其身分時，可以把它當普通名詞，加上冠詞。

USAGE PRACTICE

▶ "**A** Mr. David Johnson has called to see you, sir," the maid said.

女佣説：「先生，有一位大衛・強森先生打電話來説要見您。」

▶ My father has gone to dinner with **a** Mr. White. 我爸爸已經和一位懷特先生去吃晚餐了。

▶ **A** Mrs. Jones has just moved in next door. 一位瓊斯太太剛搬進隔壁。

▶ The news says that **a** Mr. Ross has won the first prize. "I wonder if it is **the** Mr. Ross we know," Jane said.

新聞報導説有一位羅斯先生贏得頭獎。珍説：「我想知道那是否是我們認識的羅斯先生。」

> **但是我們會用** ▶ Mr. Brown is the father of four children. 布朗先生是四個小孩的父親。
>
> ★已確定布朗先生的身分，故 Mr. Brown 前不加冠詞。

(g) 複數可數名詞、不可數名詞或抽象名詞前，不可加不定冠詞 a 或 an。

USAGE PRACTICE

rice 米   water 水   bread 麵包   meat 肉

▶ Beauty lies in the eye of the beholder. 情人眼中出西施。(×A beauty...)

▶ We can buy eggs and butter from the farm.

我們可以在這農場買雞蛋和奶油。(×...an eggs and a butter...)

▶ Simplicity is the best virtue. 簡樸是最高尚的美德。(×A simplicity...)

▶ The tree is laden with pears. 這棵樹結滿梨子。(×...a pears.)

▶ Sand has got into my shoes. 沙子掉進我的鞋子裡。(×A sand...)

▶ Honesty is the best policy. 誠實為上策。(×An honesty...)

1-3 定冠詞 (the)

(a) 定冠詞 the 置於有片語或子句修飾的特定人或事物之前。

USAGE PRACTICE

▶ This is **the** cat which caught the rat.　這就是抓到那隻老鼠的貓。

▶ I'm going to **the** bus stop near the market.　我要去市場附近的公車站。

▶ This is **the** bicycle I borrowed from Paul.　這就是我向保羅借來的腳踏車。

▶ **The** man who came here yesterday is here again.　昨天來這裡的那個人又來了。

▶ Let's go to **the** swimming pool in Sunshine Park.　我們去陽光公園的游泳池吧。

▶ This is **the** book I was telling you about.　這就是我跟你說過的那本書。

▶ He wants **the** bottle that is on top of the cupboard.　他想要櫥櫃上面的那個瓶子。

▶ **The** book you wanted to buy is out of stock.　你要買的書已經沒有現貨了。

▶ **The** boy that you spoke to is my brother.　和你講話的那個男孩是我的弟弟。

▶ I'd like to speak to **the** man who owns this place.　我想要和擁有這地方的人說話。

▶ **The** woman who talked to me just now is the wife of the Minister of Foreign Affairs.
剛才跟我說話的女子是外交部長的妻子。

(b) 定冠詞 the 置於第二次被提及的人、事、物之前。

USAGE PRACTICE

▶ There is **a** chair in the garden. **The** chair is under the tree.
花園裡有一張椅子，那張椅子就在樹底下。

▶ His bicycle had **a** puncture. He pushed **the** bicycle to a shop to have **the** puncture
repaired.　他的腳踏車輪胎被刺破一個洞，他把那腳踏車推到店裡去把那個洞補起來。

▶ She found **a** needle in **a** box. **The** needle was old and rusty; so was **the** box.
她在一個盒子裡找到一根針。那根針很舊而且生鏽，那個盒子也一樣。

(c) 定冠詞 the 置於獨一無二的事物之前，例如海洋、海灣、河流、群島、山脈（但
非單獨的山）等的名稱，或含有 united、republic 或 union 的某些國名。

USAGE PRACTICE

---

the sun 太陽	**the** earth 地球	**the** moon 月亮
the sea 海	**the** sky 天空	**the** tide 潮水
the equator 赤道	**the** horizon 地平線	**the** weather 天氣
the world 世界	**the** Atlantic Ocean 大西洋	**the** Congo River 剛果河
the East 東方	**the** Himalayas 喜瑪拉雅山	**the** Philippines 菲律賓
the North Pole 北極	**the** Bay of Bengal 孟加拉灣	

the United States of America 美國　　　**the** Hawaiian Islands 夏威夷群島

▶ **The** earth moves around **the** sun. 地球繞著太陽運轉。

▶ **The** Himalayas are an extension of **the** Pamir Knot. 喜瑪拉雅山脈是帕米爾山結的延伸。

▶ **The** Andes are an important mountain range on **the** South American continent.
安地斯山脈是南美洲大陸的重要山脈。

▶ Look at **the** Fiji Islands in **the** Pacific Ocean. 看看在太平洋中的斐濟群島。

▶ **The** River Nile flows into **the** Mediterranean Sea. 尼羅河注入地中海。

▶ **The** Great Wall is in China. 萬里長城位於中國。

▶ **The** Suez Canal belongs to Egypt. 蘇伊士運河屬於埃及。

(d) 定冠詞 the 置於最高級形容詞或序數詞之前。

USAGE PRACTICE

the best 最好的　　　　**the** loudest 最大聲的　　　　**the** most beautiful 最美麗的

▶ **The** most expensive object is not necessarily the best. 最貴的東西不一定是最好的。

▶ He is **the** worst batsman I have ever met. 他是我見過最差勁的板球打擊手。

▶ **The** highest mountain in this region is Mt. Misty. 這地區最高的山是霧山。

▶ London is one of **the** busiest cities in the world. 倫敦是世界上最繁忙的城市之一。

▶ She was **the** first woman from here to become a doctor. 她是出自這裡的第一位女醫生。

▶ **The** last person who saw him was his wife. 最後一個見到他的人是他的太太。

(e) 在名詞前加上定冠詞 the，來表示最高級的涵義。其真正意義要看上下文而定。

USAGE PRACTICE

▶ Winston Churchill has been called **the** man of the century.
溫士頓·邱吉爾被譽為世紀偉人。(the man 的意思是 the greatest man)

▶ This is **the** job for you. 這就是最適合你的工作。（the job 的意思是 the most suitable job）

▶ She is **the** girl for him. 她是他的真命天女。（the girl 的意思是 the best girl）

(f) 定冠詞 the 也可指同一類別的人或物，用於表示全體的單數名詞之前。

USAGE PRACTICE

▶ **The** mango is a tropical fruit. 芒果是一種熱帶水果。

▶ **The** crab belongs to a group of animals called "crustaceans." 螃蟹屬於甲殼綱動物。

▶ **The** lion is the king of the beasts. 獅子是萬獸之王。

▶ Society respects **the** honest person. 社會尊重誠實的人。

(g) 定冠詞 the 可以放在形容詞前，表示某一種人的全體。

USAGE PRACTICE

▶ **The** poor should be given help. 窮人應該被幫助。

（the poor 相當於 the poor people）

▶ **The** brilliant always pass their examinations.

聰明的學生總能通過考試。（the brilliant 相當於 the brilliant students）

▶ **The** good will be rewarded. 好人會有好報。（the good 相當於 the good people）

(h) 定冠詞 the 也可以加上形容詞或副詞的比較級，表示「越…就越…」。

USAGE PRACTICE

▶ **The** more, **the** merrier. 人越多越歡樂。

▶ **The** higher the score, **the** better. 分數越高越好。

▶ **The** more he has, **the** more he wants. 他擁有的越多，想要的就越多。

1-4 零冠詞

(a) 在表示全體的普通名詞、物質名詞或抽象名詞前不用冠詞。

USAGE PRACTICE

▶ Man must eat to live. 人類必須進食以維生。(×The man...)

▶ Thailand exports rice to many countries. 泰國出口稻米到許多國家。(×...the rice...)

▶ Friendship is worth more than gold. 友誼的價值勝於黃金。(×The friendship...the gold.)

▶ Honor should be cherished. 榮譽應該被珍惜。(×An honor...)

▶ Pride goes before a fall. 驕者必敗。(×A pride...)

(b) 運動、城鎮、州、國家、單獨的一座山、島嶼或湖泊的名稱前面不必加冠詞。

USAGE PRACTICE

▶ We play badminton. 我們打羽毛球。

▶ Venice is a big city in Italy. 威尼斯是義大利的一個大城市。

▶ We planned to go to Tokyo for the holidays. 我們計畫去東京渡假。

▶ He lives in Australia. 他住在澳洲。

▶ It comes from Japan. 它來自日本。

▶ Madagascar is an island in the Indian Ocean off the southeastern coast of Africa.

馬達加斯加是位於非洲東南海岸外,印度洋上的一個島嶼。

 但是,當上述專有名詞轉為形容詞(或具有形容詞性),後接名詞時,則需要加冠詞。另外,當上述專有名詞含有介系詞 of 或表示「像⋯的地方」時,則轉為普通名詞,前面可以加冠詞。

▶ We have **a** badminton court. 我們有個羽毛球場。

▶ He is **an** Australian boy. 他是個澳洲籍的男孩。

▶ It is **a** Japanese product. 它是個日本產品。

▶ The team came from Newtown. **The** Newtown team won. 這隊伍來自新城,新城隊獲勝。

▶ John lives in Heaven Bay. He is hurrying to catch **the** Heaven Bay bus now.

約翰住在天堂灣,他現在正趕著要搭前往天堂灣的公車。

▶ **The** Venice of the East is Bangkok. 東方威尼斯是曼谷。

▶ **The** Isle of Man is in the Irish Sea. 曼島位於愛爾蘭海。

(c) 在三餐之前不使用冠詞。

USAGE PRACTICE

▶ After breakfast, we set out on our journey. 早餐過後,我們出發去旅行。

▶ We will have lunch in that restaurant. 我們將在那家餐廳吃午飯。

▶ They went to the movies after dinner. 他們在晚餐後去看電影。

但是，提及特定的一餐時，可以使用冠詞。

▶ I went to **the** lunch given in honor of the manager yesterday. 我昨天參加向經理致敬的午餐。

▶ **A** staff dinner will be held next week. 下週將會舉行一場員工晚宴。

▶ They are going to give **a** dinner to celebrate his victory. 他們將要舉辦一個晚宴來慶祝他的勝利。

(d) 某些疾病如 cholera（霍亂）、malaria（瘧疾）、typhoid（傷寒）等名詞前都不必加冠詞。

USAGE PRACTICE

▶ Cholera spread rapidly through the town. 霍亂很快地在這城鎮中擴散。

▶ My sister is ill; she has influenza. 我姊姊生病了，她得了流行性感冒。

▶ Children usually have chicken pox at this age. 小孩常在這個年紀長水痘。

▶ Measles can be a dangerous disease. 麻疹可能會是種危險的疾病。

 但是，在 flu（流行性感冒）之前可以用定冠詞 the，在 cold（感冒）、fever（發燒）、headache（頭痛）、ulcer（潰瘍）和 cramp（痙攣）等字之前可以用不定冠詞 a 或 an。

▶ Both their children are down with **the** flu. 他們的兩個孩子都得了流行性感冒。

▶ He had **a** cramp while he was swimming. 他游泳時，抽筋了。

▶ I am not suffering form **a** cold, but I do have **a** fever and **a** headache.
我沒有感冒，但是我的確有發燒和頭痛。

(e) 學校、市場、教堂、醫院、法院或監獄等地方的名詞，如果不是單純指特定的地方，而是要表達在該地點會行使的動作時，前面通常不必加冠詞。

USAGE PRACTICE

▶ She goes to school by bus. 她搭公車上學。

▶ He was sent to prison for robbery. 他因搶劫而入獄。

▶ He has been in prison for the past two years. 過去兩年他入獄服刑。

▶ You must be home by half past ten. 你十點半前一定要回到家。

▶ It is getting late; I must return home. 時候不早了，我必須回家去。

▶ The quarreling parties brought their case to court. 這爭吵的一夥人向法院提出訴訟。

▶ The Smiths go to church every Sunday. 史密斯一家人每個星期天都上教堂做禮拜。

▶ You should be in bed by now. 你現在應該上床睡覺了。

但是，上述表示地方的名詞如果指一個特定的地方，則必須用冠詞。

▶ He parks his car in front of **the** school. 他把車停在這學校前面。
▶ There is a bus stop near **the** church. 這教堂附近有個公車站。
▶ **The** prison was burned down during the war. 這監獄在戰爭期間燒毀了。
▶ The accident took place in front of **the** court. 這意外在法院前發生。
▶ I made **the** bed and went downstairs for breakfast. 我整理床舖，然後下樓吃早餐。

(f) 道路的名稱前不必加冠詞。

USAGE PRACTICE

▶ I live on Brewster Road. 我住在布魯斯特路上。

 但是，在下列情況中，道路已經是小寫的普通名詞，故前面必須加冠詞。

▶ High Street is **a** busy road. 高街是一條繁忙的道路。
▶ They are repairing certain parts of **the** road. 他們正在修理這條路的某些部份。
▶ **The** coast road was closed to traffic. 這海岸公路封閉無法通行。

(g) 語言或運動的名稱之前不用冠詞。

USAGE PRACTICE

▶ Tagalog is the official language of the Philippines. 塔加拉語是菲律賓的官方語言。

▶ Badminton is a popular game. 羽毛球是流行的運動。

 但是，當語言或運動的名稱被當作形容詞，後接名詞時，就要加冠詞。

▶ I play badminton. I bought **a** badminton racket. 我打羽毛球。我買了一支羽毛球球拍。
▶ She speaks German fluently as she has **a** German tutor.
她的德語說很流利，因為她有一位德文家教。
▶ Pauline studies Chinese in the university, and she enjoys teaching her friends Hokkien, which is **a** Chinese dialect. 寶琳在大學學中文，她喜歡教她的朋友說福建話——一種中文方言。

(h) kind、sort、type（用來表示種類）接介系詞 of 後的名詞之前，不用冠詞。

USAGE PRACTICE

▶ What kind of bird is this? 這是哪種鳥？

> ▶ What <u>sort of paper</u> do you want? 你要哪種紙？

> ▶ What <u>type of animal</u> is that? 那是哪種動物？

Chapter 1　應用練習

PART 1

請在空格中填入冠詞 a、an 或 the。若不需要加上冠詞，請打×。

1. _____ football match
2. _____ honest man
3. _____ hopeless task
4. _____ measles
5. _____ weather
6. _____ National Day
7. _____ exciting match
8. _____ united army
9. _____ Park Avenue
10. _____ south
11. _____ headache
12. play _____ baseball
13. _____ Federal Highway
14. _____ farmer
15. _____ Himalayas
16. _____ 'u'
17. _____ broken arm
18. _____ beginning
19. _____ eye surgeon
20. have _____ breakfast
21. _____ Lake Gardens
22. _____ smallest particle
23. _____ influenza
24. _____ Madura Island
25. _____ uniformed guard
26. _____ Aleutian Islands
27. _____ hot sun
28. _____ hour's time
29. _____ New York
30. _____ wedding dinner

PART 2

請在空格中填入冠詞 a、an 或 the。若不需要加上冠詞，請打×。

1. As he was coming back from _____ school, he met with _____ accident.

2. One of _____ spectators phoned for _____ ambulance and _____ police.

3. _____ captain of _____ football team has resigned. No one knows _____ reason for his resignation.

4. _____ airplane just flew over our house. _____ noise woke _____ baby up.

5. She poured _____ cup of coffee for herself and went to relax in _____ sitting room.

6. _____ moon was at its fullest last night. _____ weather was fine, too.

7. We went for _____ walk right after _____ dinner.

8. She shut _____ windows to prevent _____ rain from coming into _____ room.

9. This country has _____ hot, wet climate with _____ plenty of _____ sun and

_____ rain _____ whole year round.

10. He is _____ salesman in _____ agricultural firm.

11. She is going to cut _____ most beautiful flowers in _____ garden to decorate _____ house for _____ grand occasion.

12. He lives in _____ bungalow at _____ top of _____ hill.

13. Where is _____ piece of _____ cloth I bought this afternoon?

14. _____ hotel offers you _____ best food at _____ moderate price.

PART 3

請在空格中填入冠詞 a、an 或 the。若不需要加上冠詞，請打×。

1. There is a cart over there. Please push _____ cart into _____ sitting room.

2. They say _____ monkeys are very intelligent _____ animals.

3. There is _____ fly in _____ soup. Don't drink it.

4. I have _____ question to ask you, and I expect _____ answer from you.

5. He took up _____ swimming as _____ hobby last year. He says that it is _____ best form of exercise.

6. They have been at _____ work since five in _____ morning. Ask _____ office boy to bring in _____ drinks for them. They deserve _____ rest now.

7. _____ lawyer, _____ businessman, and _____ engineer appeared together in the program on _____ television last night.

8. Here is a pill. If you take _____ pill now, you will not feel any pain afterward. Meanwhile, I'll make _____ appointment for you with _____ doctor.

9. He had _____ lunch with _____ old friend.

10. _____ year consists of 365 days. _____ leap year occurs every _____ four years. There is _____ extra day in _____ leap year.

11. _____ Swift River is _____ chief means of communication to _____ interior of that country, and all _____ large towns situated on its banks.

12. Look at _____ fish dealer. He is packing _____ fish into _____ boxes filled with _____ ice.

13. _____ old man wearing _____ pair of spectacles asked me _____ way to _____ People's Park yesterday.

PART 4

請在空格中填入冠詞 a、an 或 the。若不需要加上冠詞，請打×。

1. Seagull Bay is situated at _____ southernmost tip of _____ Emerald Isle.

2. The man took out a sack. He emptied _____ sack and filled it with _____ sugar. Then, he sealed _____ sack and carried it to _____ back of _____ shop.

3. Christmas Island lies about 500 kilometers south of _____ Sunda Straits. It is now under _____ control of _____ Australian Government.

4. "_____ apple of discord" is _____ idiomatic expression meaning "_____ subject of envy and strife."

5. Some people say you must not take _____ medicine on _____ empty stomach. _____ best time for you to take medicine is after you have had _____ meal.

6. _____ monetary unit of _____ Great Britain is _____ pound.

7. _____ wigwam is _____ tent or _____ hut which is made by putting skins or mats over _____ framework of poles.

8. He does not wish to be under _____ obligation to anyone. He is going to do _____ whole job by himself.

9. He lost _____ eye when he was very young and had to be fitted with _____ false one.

10. Your shirt has _____ oil stain on it. You had better soak _____ shirt in _____ soapy water when we get back to _____ house.

11. He usually smokes _____ pipe, but sometimes he smokes _____ cigarettes. He can smoke _____ packet of cigarettes in _____ day.

12. She has already written _____ letter, but she is still searching for _____ envelope and _____ stamp.

13. She is paying fifty dollars _____ day for _____ room in _____ hotel she is staying at. It is _____ air-conditioned room with _____ bathroom attached to it.

14. _____ 'o' and _____ 'x' are probably _____ easiest letters to write.

15. _____ population of that country is about 920,000 with _____ youths forming roughly _____ three-quarters of _____ total.

PART 5

請在空格中填入冠詞 a、an 或 the。若不需要加上冠詞，請打×。

1. There is _____ old man walking down _____ road. He has _____ walking stick in one hand and _____ hat in _____ other.

2. _____ insect has six _____ legs, but _____ spider has eight. _____ spider is not _____ insect.

3. _____ uncle of mine is coming to stay for _____ week. He is bringing _____ Mr. Drew with him. We don't know the man, but we will prepare _____ guest rooms for them.

4. A circus has come to _____ town. I saw the procession of _____ animals along _____ Rosario Avenue. There were _____ elephants and _____ horses. _____ clown was distributing free _____ tickets.

5. _____ workers in the factory were often mistreated and exploited. Therefore, they decided to form _____ workers'union. As _____ united body, they have more _____ power and _____ strength to overcome _____ difficulties.

6. Yesterday, _____ European man came up to me and asked me _____ way to _____ New Town. I told him to take _____ old Airport Road and turn left at _____ first intersection.

7. _____ accident occurred at _____ main road near _____ Grand View Cinema. _____ motorist knocked down _____ pedestrian. _____ motorist was driving his car at seventy kilometers _____ hour, which was beyond _____ speed limit.

8. _____ Andes are _____ range of mountains on _____ western side of _____ South America.

9. She had been waiting for _____ hour at _____ hotel, but there was still no sign of _____ Indian carpet seller.

10. We went to play _____ tennis at her house, but we went _____ home when it started to rain.

11. _____ rain did not stop for many _____ days. _____ Pearl River flooded its banks, and _____ water was flowing rapidly.

12. _____ Aleutian Islands are _____ chain of islands extending westward from _____ southern tip of _____ Alaskan Peninsula.

13. I have _____ pen pal in _____ United Kingdom. She is _____ nurse in one of

_____ best hospitals there. Only _____ seriously ill go there for treatment.

14. _____ Mrs. Baker wants to see _____ manager. I have taken her to _____ office, but _____ manager is not around. _____ woman is waiting outside now.

15. Don't go near her. She has _____ chicken pox. _____ doctor told her not to go out, but she is _____ disobedient girl.

16. Mrs. Green is going to _____ market. _____ market is on _____ River Road, just over _____ bridge.

17. _____ unknown always intrigue _____ curious person. He will never be satisfied until he has got to _____ bottom of it.

18. _____ sun was shining fiercely, and there was not _____ cloud in _____ sky. _____ earth was parched and cracked in some _____ places.

PART 6

請在空格中填入冠詞 a、an 或 the。若不需要加上冠詞，請打 × 。

1. We went to _____ show at _____ Faber Cinema. _____ beginning of _____ show was quite dull, but it became exciting toward _____ end.

2. Ann's mother works as _____ nurse in _____ General Hospital.

3. _____ climate here is warmer than that on _____ Mainland because we are near _____ equator.

4. _____ heat is intolerable sometimes, but _____ people in the country are quite used to it.

5. There is _____ cholera epidemic in _____ town. None of _____ passengers on _____ ship are allowed to get off.

6. After _____ excellent meal, we had _____ short rest before continuing _____ journey.

7. _____ disease is spreading fast, and _____ government is doing all it can to prevent the situation from getting worse.

8. "Alice, I am going to _____ church now. When my father wakes up, tell him that _____ Mr. Harris rang him up _____ hour ago," I told _____ maid.

9. _____ Leas are having _____ dinner in _____ dining room now. _____ Mrs. Lea is carrying in _____ big bowl of _____ chicken soup.

10. This is _____ best book I have read so far.

11. _____ East Indies are _____ group of _____ islands in _____ Pacific Ocean.

12. I will meet you at _____ shop near _____ junction intersection of _____ Prince Street and _____ Mayfair Road.

13. What _____ pity! Kevin has _____ bad cold and cannot go on _____ picnic with us.

14. They were trapped in _____ cave when _____ tide came in. It was nearly _____ hour later that we found them.

15. Do you know _____ area of _____ Republic of _____ Ireland?

PART 7

請在空格中填入冠詞 a、an 或 the。若不需要加上冠詞，請打✕。

1. I opened _____ door and found _____ old man wearing _____ hat standing on _____ doorstep.

2. All of them had _____ picnic near _____ waterfall at _____ Green Valley on _____ Saturday.

3. _____ boy came cycling down _____ street and banged into a tree in front of _____ house opposite ours.

4. It's _____ pity that _____ Eric could not go to _____ football match that was held on _____ school field. It was really _____ exciting game.

5. _____ price of _____ eggs has been on _____ increase for _____ long time. Now, _____ egg costs much more.

6. I found _____ empty can by _____ roadside just now. This is not _____ unusual thing, but _____ point is that _____ can may cause _____ serious accident.

7. _____ author of this book came to our school yesterday and gave us _____ lecture on _____ importance of reading good books for _____ education.

8. When I woke up early in _____ morning, I saw _____ fine mist covering _____ hills and trees. But _____ hour later, _____ mist had disappeared, and _____ sun was shining brightly.

9. As he was going to _____ school, he met with _____ accident. He had _____ bad bump on _____ head and was taken to _____ hospital in _____ ambulance.

10. _____ bus stopped at _____ bus station. _____ old woman wearing _____ faded skirt and _____ old blouse got off _____ bus.

11. Mary suddenly let out _____ frightened scream. She had felt _____ cold object brush past her face. We told her that it was probably _____ owl or _____ bat, and warned her to look out for potholes along _____ path.

12. _____ old shopkeeper works too hard in _____ shop. He is on his feet _____ whole day long, serving _____ customers, and climbing up and down _____ stepladder to get _____ things they want. What he needs is _____ long rest and _____ assistant to help him in _____ shop.

13. She sent _____ note to her cousin, telling him that she was in _____ great danger and that she needed _____ help. When he got to her house, he found that all _____ lights had been switched off. _____ only light came from _____ single candle standing on _____ table in _____ center of _____ hall.

14. I brought along _____ loaf of bread and _____ can of sardines for my lunch. I also had _____ apple, _____ orange, and _____ tomato. But I forgot to bring along _____ knife and _____ can opener. So, I ate only _____ apple, _____ orange, and _____ tomato for _____ lunch.

Chapter 2 名　詞

2-1 名詞的格

(a) 單數名詞後加 's，以形成所有格。

USAGE PRACTICE

Eddie**'s** bicycle　艾迪的腳踏車

Fanny**'s** uncle　芬妮的叔叔

the boy**'s** sister　這男孩的妹妹

the lady**'s** purse　這女士的皮包

the woman**'s** house　這女人的房子

the cat**'s** paw　這隻貓的爪子

the dog**'s** eyes　這隻狗的眼睛

Mary**'s** necklace　瑪麗的項鍊

the child**'s** toy　這孩子的玩具

the girl**'s** bag　這女孩的手提包

the man**'s** shirt　這男子的襯衫

the chicken**'s** wings　這隻雞的翅膀

the cow**'s** tail　這隻母牛的尾巴

the duck**'s** beak　這隻鴨子的喙

▶ The girl**'s** purse was stolen yesterday.　這女孩的錢包昨天被偷了。

▶ Look! The lizard**'s** tail has fallen off.　看！這隻蜥蜴的尾巴掉了。

▶ They found a man**'s** hat in the drain.　他們在排水溝裡發現一頂男帽。

(b) 以子音 s 結尾的單數名詞後加 's，以形成所有格。

USAGE PRACTICE

▶ The actress**'s** dress was beautiful.　這女演員的服裝很漂亮。

▶ The teacher was proud of the class**'s** record.　這老師以這班學生的成績為榮。

 但是，有時因為加上 's 後會造成發音上的困難，所以有時只加所有格符號 '，形成所有格。

a waitress' job　女服務生的工作

an actress' role　女演員的角色

Keats' poems　濟慈的詩

Mr. Jones' son　瓊斯先生的兒子

James' book　詹姆士的書

the princess' jewels　這公主的珠寶

Moses' Laws　摩西的法典

Charles' car　查爾斯的車子

▶ He bought a volume of Keats' poetry.　他買了一冊濟慈的詩集。

▶ Francis' mother came to my house last night.　法蘭西斯的母親昨晚來我家。

▶ Did you borrow James' book for me?　你替我借了詹姆士的書嗎？

▶ I have been to Charles' house several times.　我曾經去過查爾斯的家幾次。

(c) 字尾非 s 的複數名詞必須加 's，以形成所有格。

USAGE PRACTICE

children**'s** toys 孩子們的玩具   headmen**'s** roles 隊長們的角色

women**'s** shoes 女鞋   women**'s** dresses 女裝

men**'s** hats 男帽   men**'s** shirts 男衫

policemen**'s** parade 警員遊行   policewomen**'s** uniform 女警制服

▶ The children**'s** party was interesting. 孩子們的派對很有趣。

▶ We have not seen the new policemen**'s** uniforms yet. 我們還沒見過新的警察制服。

▶ There are women**'s** clothes for sale. 有女裝出售。

(d) 字尾是 s 的複數名詞後只須加所有格符號 '，形成所有格。

USAGE PRACTICE

rabbits' teeth 兔子的牙齒   birds' nests 鳥巢

boys' desks 男孩們的書桌   girls' laughter 女孩們的笑聲

teachers' room 教師室   ladies' handbags 女用手提包

the bridesmaids' dresses 這些伴娘們的衣服   babies' cries 嬰兒們的哭聲

princesses' jewels 公主們的珠寶   soldiers' rifles 士兵的來福槍

the Browns' house 布朗家的房子   the Wilsons' garden 威爾森家的花園

▶ The pupils' behavior made him angry. 這些學生們的行為讓他生氣。

▶ There will be a teachers' meeting this afternoon. 今天下午將召開教師會議。

▶ The women were talking about their husbands' jobs.

這些婦女正在討論她們丈夫的工作。

▶ The thief stole the twins' watches. 小偷偷走了這對雙胞胎的手錶。

(e) 沒有生命的東西不可以用所有格符號 '，須用介系詞片語「of + the + 名詞」，形成所有格。

USAGE PRACTICE

the handle **of** the pail 這桶子的把手   the lid **of** the box 這箱子的蓋子

the pedals **of** the bicycle 這腳踏車的踏板   the wheels **of** the car 這汽車的車輪

the keys **of** the piano 這鋼琴的琴鍵	the hands **of** the clock 這時鐘的指針
the pages **of** the book 這本書的內頁	the colors **of** the rainbow 這彩虹的顏色
the leaves **of** the plant 這植物的葉子	the branches **of** the tree 這樹的樹枝
the legs **of** the chair 這椅子的腳	the windows **of** the house 這房屋的窗戶
the time **of** the meeting 這會議的時間	the noise **of** the traffic 交通的噪音
the top **of** the cupboard 這櫥櫃的頂部	the rim **of** the glass 這玻璃杯的杯緣

 注意　但是，有一些例外情況，表示時間、容量、價值、距離、重量等的名詞可以直接加 's 或只加所有格符號 '，以形成所有格。

an hour**'s** delay 一小時的延誤	two week**s'** rest 兩個星期的休息
a month**'s** holiday 一個月的假期	a year**'s** time 一年的時間
a day**'s** journey 一天的旅程	twenty minute**s'** walk 二十分鐘的路程
two meter**s'** distance 兩公尺的距離	two kilometer**s'** walk 兩公里的路程
yesterday**'s** paper 昨天的報紙	a dollar**'s** worth 一元的價值

▶ We will be there in an hour**'s** time. 我們一個小時內將會到那裡。
▶ After a week**'s** delay, they finally started working on it.
　 在延遲了一個星期後，他們終於開始做那件事。
▶ Ten month**s'** work was wasted. 十個月的工作白費了。
▶ Buy me a dollar**'s** worth of cookies. 替我買一塊錢的餅乾。

(f) 唯一存在的無生命名詞也可以加 's，以形成所有格。

USAGE PRACTICE	
the sun**'s** rays 太陽的光線	the earth**'s** origin 地球的起源
the moon**'s** surface 月亮的表面	the planet**'s** orbit 這行星的軌道
Australia**'s** economy 澳洲的經濟	

(g) 複合字被視為一個字，在最後一個字後加上 's，以形成所有格。

USAGE PRACTICE	
the sales clerk**'s** pay 店員的薪水	his mother-in-law**'s** house 他岳母的房子
somebody else**'s** mistakes 其他人的錯誤	the commander in chief**'s** orders 總司令的命令

(h) 任何能獨立使用的數字或字母加上 's，以形成所有格。

USAGE PRACTICE

▶ You must mind your p**'s** and q**'s**. 你必須謹言慎行。

▶ Dot your i**'s** and cross your t**'s**. 要仔細些。

▶ The three R**'s** should be taught to every child. 基本三 R 能力必須教給每個孩童。

▶ Your 3**'s** look like 8**'s**. 你寫的 3 看起來像 8。

(i) and 連接兩個名詞，表示「共同擁有」時，只在第二個名詞後加 's。

USAGE PRACTICE

my father and mother**'s** friends 我爸媽（共同的）朋友

(j) 許多慣用語也使用所有格。

USAGE PRACTICE

New Year**'s** Eve 新年的前夕（除夕）　　at my wits**'** end 不知所措

for peace**'s** sake 為了和平　　for goodnes**s'** sake 看在老天爺的份上

for conscience**'s** sake 為了良心　　for justice**'s** sake 為了正義

out of harm**'s** way 遠離危險　　one**'s** heart**'s** desire 心中渴望的東西

a stone**'s** throw 投石可及的距離（很近的距離）

(k) 為了要避免冗長且不自然的片語，即使是人的所有格，也可以使用表示所有格的
介系詞 of 來取代。

USAGE PRACTICE

the director of the Home for the Aged's plan （冗長且不自然）

→ the plan of the director of the Home for the Aged 老人之家的執行長的計畫

 小練習

請利用 's、' 或 of... 將下列各題改為所有格的型態。

1. the monkeys/tails → ＿＿＿＿＿＿＿＿　　2. the mountain/the foot → ＿＿＿＿＿＿＿＿

3. Francis/new car → ＿＿＿＿＿＿＿＿　　4. the needle/the eye → ＿＿＿＿＿＿＿＿

5. a minute/pause → ＿＿＿＿＿＿＿＿　　6. the earth/the movement → ＿＿＿＿＿＿＿＿

7. her brother-in-law/car → _____   8. the examination/the results → _____

9. wolves/howling → _____   10. Ari/message → _____

11. the heiress/jewels → _____   12. the judge/decision → _____

13. the line/the end → _____   14. the chairman/speech → _____

15. the stars/twinkling → _____   16. the secretary/salary → _____

17. the tourists/luggage → _____   18. the river/the source → _____

19. my niece/toys → _____   20. two months/absence → _____

21. the policemen/hats → _____   22. the flowers/the colors → _____

23. London/position → _____   24. the bees/stings → _____

25. the box/the sides → _____   26. the body/needs → _____

27. the moon/surface → _____   28. the jug/the rim → _____

29. the workers/union → _____   30. two dollars/worth → _____

☞ 更多相關習題請見本章應用練習 Part 1～Part 7。

2-2 名詞的數

(a) 一般名詞的字尾加 s，以形成複數。

USAGE PRACTICE

book**s** 書	table**s** 餐桌	page**s** 頁
girl**s** 女孩	letter**s** 信件	building**s** 建築物
act**s** 行為	chair**s** 椅子	machine**s** 機器
orange**s** 橘子	game**s** 比賽	shop**s** 商店
servant**s** 僕人	astronaut**s** 太空人	drawer**s** 抽屜

(b) 名詞的字尾是 s、sh、ch 或 x 時，加 es，以形成複數。

USAGE PRACTICE

class**es** 班級	pass**es** 通行證	dress**es** 衣裳
bus**es** 公車	dish**es** 盤子	wish**es** 願望
brush**es** 刷子	switch**es** 開關	bench**es** 長凳
watch**es** 手錶	torch**es** 火把	branch**es** 樹枝

boxes 盒子	taxes 稅金	sexes 性別

(c) 名詞的字尾是 o 時，大多加 es，以形成複數。

USAGE PRACTICE		
mangoes 芒果	buffaloes 水牛	heroes 英雄
mosquitoes 蚊子	Negroes 黑人	potatoes 馬鈴薯

但是我們會用 ▶ pianos 鋼琴　　　photos 照片　　　radios 收音機

★此類用法並無特殊規則，必須直接記憶。

(d) 名詞的字尾是 y 時，去 y 加 ies，以形成複數。

USAGE PRACTICE		
lady → ladies 女士	baby → babies 嬰兒	ferry → ferries 渡輪
army → armies 軍隊	pony → ponies 小馬	butterfly → butterflies 蝴蝶
spy → spies 間諜	fly → flies 蒼蠅	city → cities 城市
navy → navies 海軍艦隊	mystery → mysteries 神秘的事物	

但是我們會用 ▶ valleys 山谷　　　days 日子　　　highways 公路
boys 男孩　　　monkeys 猴子

★但若 y 之前為母音時，則仍然是直接加 s 即可。

(e) 名詞的字尾是 f 或 fe 者，去掉 f 或 fe 加 ves，以形成複數。

USAGE PRACTICE		
shelf → shelves 架子	calf → calves 小牛	knife → knives 刀子
leaf → leaves 樹葉	wife → wives 妻子	

但是我們會用 ▶ chiefs 首領　　　roofs 屋頂　　　gulfs 海灣
hoofs （牛、馬的）蹄

★此類用法並無特殊規則，必須直接記憶。

(f) 有些名詞的複數形是不規則變化，必須以不同的方式（如改變母音或加上 e、x 等）形成複數。

man → men 男子	woman → women 女人	child → children 兒童
tooth → teeth 牙齒	goose → geese 鵝	foot → feet 腳
ox → oxen 公牛	mouse → mice 老鼠	louse → lice 蝨子
fungus → fungi 菌類	cactus → cacti 仙人掌	locus → loci 所在地
radius → radii 半徑	formula → formulae 公式	larva → larvae 幼蟲
nebula → nebulae 星雲	crisis → crises 危機	oasis → oases 綠洲
stratum → strata 地層	medium → media 媒體	
bureau → bureaux/bureaus 局	tableau → tableaux/tableaus 戲劇性的場面	

(g) 有些名詞單複數同形。

USAGE PRACTICE

sheep → sheep 綿羊	deer → deer 鹿	fish → fish 魚
swine → swine 豬	cod → cod 鱈魚	fruit → fruit 水果
salmon → salmon 鮭魚	Chinese → Chinese 中國人	aircraft → aircraft 航空器

(h) 有些名詞只有單數用法，沒有複數形。

USAGE PRACTICE

furniture 傢俱	traffic 交通	information 資訊
clothing 衣物	audience 觀眾	advice 忠告
baggage/luggage 行李	intelligence 智慧	vegetation 植物（總稱）
knowledge 知識	laughter 笑聲	equipment 設備器材
machinery 機械		

 有些名詞雖然是單數形，但表示複數涵義。

police 警方   people 人們

(i) 有些名詞只有複數用法，沒有單數形。

USAGE PRACTICE

clothes 衣服	trousers 褲子	spectacles 眼鏡
scissors 剪刀	shears 大剪刀	pliers 鉗子
knickers 燈籠褲	dominoes 骨牌遊戲	

注意 有些名詞雖作複數形，但表示單數涵義。

mumps 腮腺炎	politics 政治	news 新聞

(j) 複合字則改變其主要字，以形成複數。

USAGE PRACTICE

machine gun → machine gun**s** 機關槍	pen holder → pen holder**s** 筆筒
runner-up → runner**s**-up 亞軍	passer-by → passer**s**-by 路人
looker-on → looker**s**-on 旁觀者	prisoner of war → prisoner**s** of war 戰俘
brother-in-law → brother**s**-in-law 姊夫	son-in-law → son**s**-in-law 女婿
great-aunt → great-aunt**s** 姑婆，姨婆	ticket collector → ticket collector**s** 收票員
commander in chief → commander**s** in chief 統帥	

(k) 有時，在專有名詞後也可加上 s，以形成複數，作普通名詞。

USAGE PRACTICE

the Parker**s** 派克一家人	the Smith**s** 史密斯一家人	the Brown**s** 布朗一家人
two Lily**s** 兩個麗莉		

(l) 有些名詞有兩個意思稍微不同的複數形。

USAGE PRACTICE

fish（單數）→ fish（複數）泛指一般的魚

↘ fishes（複數）某特定種類的魚

people（單數）→ people（複數）人們

↘ peoples（複數）民族

(m) 有些名詞兼作可數名詞（有複數形）與不可數名詞（無複數形），且意思不同。

小練習

請寫出下列字彙的複數形。如果沒有複數形，請打×。

1. shelf _____
2. cliff _____
3. life _____
4. safe _____
5. trout _____
6. cod _____
7. loaf _____
8. oasis _____
9. information _____
10. ox _____
11. bamboo _____
12. Chinese _____
13. basis _____
14. spy _____
15. child _____
16. witch _____
17. sheep _____
18. staff _____
19. oven _____
20. advice _____
21. bread _____
22. handkerchief _____
23. formula _____
24. phenomenon _____
25. daughter-in-law _____

☞ 更多相關習題請見本章應用練習 Part 8～Part 13。

2-3 名詞的構成

(a) 某一些字加上適當的字根，有時再做點適當的變化，就可構成名詞。

USAGE PRACTICE

-ness	thick**ness** 厚度	cleanli**ness** 潔淨	great**ness** 偉大	loveli**ness** 可愛
	holi**ness** 神聖	good**ness** 善良	kind**ness** 親切	dark**ness** 黑暗
	close**ness** 接近	lazi**ness** 懶惰		
-ess	host**ess** 女主人			
-ty	safe**ty** 安全	cruel**ty** 殘忍		
-ity	stupid**ity** 愚蠢	humid**ity** 溼氣	timid**ity** 膽怯	solid**ity** 堅硬
	generos**ity** 慷慨	pur**ity** 純潔	real**ity** 事實	
-tion	produc**tion** 生產	descrip**tion** 描述	invita**tion** 邀請	atten**tion** 注意

	addition 增加 devotion 奉獻	connection 連結 creation 創造	adoption 領養	action 行動
-sion	admission 許可 invasion 侵略	permission 准許 confusion 困惑	revision 修正 conversion 轉變	decision 決定
-y -cy	entry 入口 accuracy 正確性	discovery 發現 vacancy 空缺	injury 受傷 secrecy 秘密	recovery 康復 bankruptcy 破產
-ery -ry	robbery 搶劫 bravery 勇敢	mockery 嘲笑 slavery 奴隸制度	scenery 風景 rivalry 競爭	machinery 機械
-th	width 寬度	depth 深度	growth 成長	breadth 寬度
-er -or -ar	maker 製造者 actor 演員 scholar 學者	repairer 修理工 sailor 水手 registrar 登錄者	teacher 老師 senator 參議員 beggar 乞丐	dancer 舞者 director 導演
-al -ial	approval 贊成 burial 埋葬	withdrawal 撤回 denial 否認	arrival 到達	
-ance	attendance 出席	appearance 出現	entrance 入口	assistance 幫助
-age	postage 郵資	package 包裹	marriage 婚姻	leakage 洩漏
-ant	accountant 會計	consultant 顧問	assistant 助理	attendant 侍者
-dom	freedom 自由	wisdom 智慧	boredom 無聊	kingdom 王國
-ist	guitarist 吉他手	scientist 科學家	typist 打字員	violinist 小提琴手
-ee	employee 雇員 absentee 缺席者	refugee 難民 licensee 領到執照的人	payee 收款人	referee 裁判
-an -ian	American 美國人 magician 魔術師	Asian 亞洲人 musician 音樂家	physician 醫生	
-ice	cowardice 懦弱			
-ure	pleasure 樂趣	moisture 濕氣		
-ment	argument 爭論 enjoyment 享受	contentment 滿足 movement 運動	payment 付款 engagement 保證	judgment 審判 merriment 快樂

-ism	Buddhism 佛教	heroism 英雄主義	realism 現實主義　tourism 觀光業
	idealism 理想主義	criticism 批評	terrorism 恐怖主義
-hood	falsehood 虛假	childhood 童年時期	brotherhood 手足之情
	manhood 成年期	motherhood 母性	neighborhood 鄰近地區
-ship	friendship 友誼	workmanship 工藝	leadership 領導才能
	hardship 困苦	relationship 關係	partnership 合夥關係
	kinship 親屬關係	membership 會員身份	

(b) 有些名詞的構成變化比較沒有規則。

USAGE PRACTICE

affect 影響 → effect 效果	advise 勸告 → advice 忠告	speak 說話 → speech 演說
contain 容納 → content 內容	live 活著 → life 生命	believe 相信 → belief 信仰
mix 混合 → mixture 混合物	fail 失敗 → failure 失敗	try 嘗試 → trial 試用
do 做 → deed 行為	hate 憎恨 → hatred 仇恨	proud 驕傲的 → pride 自負
weigh 秤重 → weight 重量	shade 遮蔽 → shadow 影子	sell 販賣 → sale 銷售
ascend 上升 → ascent 上升	high 高的 → height 高度	

(c) 有些字動詞與名詞同形。

USAGE PRACTICE

account 解釋 → account 解釋	taste 嚐 → taste 味覺	comfort 安慰 → comfort 安慰
attack 攻擊 → attack 攻擊	love 愛 → love 愛情	practice 練習 → practice 練習
fight 打仗 → fight 戰鬥	escort 護送 → escort 護送者	address 演講 → address 演講
rebel 反叛 → rebel 反叛者	feel 觸摸 → feel 觸覺	respect 尊敬 → respect 尊敬
laugh 笑 → laugh 笑聲	risk 冒險 → risk 冒險	center 居中 → center 中心

 許多動詞與名詞雖然同形，但發音並不同。特別是重音節的位置，名詞通常重音在前，而動詞通常重音在後。

record [ˋrɛkəd] *n.* 紀錄；唱片　[rɪˋkɔrd] *v.* 記錄
conflict [ˋkɑnflɪkt] *n.* 衝突　[kənˋflɪkt] *v.* 衝突

(d) 有些形容詞也可作為名詞。

USAGE PRACTICE
blind 遮掩物   cold 寒冷

請寫出下列字彙的名詞。

1. hard _____
2. absent _____
3. govern _____
4. develop _____
5. mental _____
6. compete _____
7. revise _____
8. wide _____
9. rich _____
10. proud _____
11. young _____
12. true _____
13. long _____
14. timid _____
15. high _____
16. oblige _____
17. vain _____
18. brutal _____
19. sudden _____
20. real _____
21. anxious _____
22. perfect _____
23. content _____
24. pleasant _____
25. angry _____

☞ 更多相關習題請見本章應用練習 Part 14～Part 18。

2-4 可數名詞和不可數名詞

(a) 可數名詞具有單數形和複數形。

USAGE PRACTICE		
egg → eggs 蛋	box → boxes 箱子	cup → cups 杯子
plant → plants 植物	bird → birds 鳥	bicycle → bicycles 腳踏車
boy → boys 男孩	chair → chairs 椅子	coin → coins 硬幣

注意 單數可數名詞不可單獨使用在句子中，必須用冠詞或不定形容詞加以描述。此外，複數可數名詞之前則可用 many、some、few、a few、a lot of、several、plenty of、a large number of... 等量詞來修飾。

▶ I saw **a** mouse running across the kitchen floor. 我看到一隻老鼠跑過廚房地板。

▶ Do you have **any** good idea? 你有任何好主意嗎？

▶ There were **many** schoolboys at the rally. 在這場大會中有許多男學童。

▶ **Several** girls decided to bake some cakes. 幾個女孩子決定要烤一些蛋糕。

▶ **A few** lives were lost during the floods. 有幾個人在洪水中喪命。

▶ **A lot of** us think that examinations should be abolished. 我們許多人認為考試應該被廢除。

(b) 不可數名詞沒有單複數形的區別。

USAGE PRACTICE		
water 水	rubbish 垃圾	coffee 咖啡
oil 油	heat 熱度	strength 力量
bread 麵包	rice 米	furniture 家具

 不可數名詞不可計算，前面不可加不定冠詞 a 或 an，必須用 much、some、a little、plenty of、a lot of、a large amount of、a great deal of... 等量詞來修飾。

▶ There is not **much** coffee in the pot. 壺裡沒有多少咖啡了。

▶ We did not see **much** dirt on the floor. 我們在地板上沒有看到很多塵土。

▶ How **much** butter is there in the refrigerator? 冰箱裡有多少奶油？

▶ There is **some** sugar in the bowl. 碗裡有一些糖。

▶ **A little** more salt is needed in the soup. 這湯須要多加一點鹽。

▶ He has a **lot of** money. 他有很多錢。

▶ **A lot of** the land has been planted with barley. 很多土地都已經種了大麥。

▶ **A large amount of** money is needed for the building. 這棟建築物需要花大筆的錢。

▶ **A great deal of** work has been put into it. 很多的心力已經投入這件事。

(c) 不可數名詞常用一些特殊的單位詞來計數。

USAGE PRACTICE		
a **cup** of sugar 一杯糖	a **block** of ice 一塊冰	a **bar** of soap 一塊肥皂
a **bowl** of soup 一碗湯	a **spoonful** of oil 一匙油	a **bottle** of water 一瓶水
a **loaf** of bread 一條麵包	a **piece** of paper 一張紙	a **slab** of stone 一片石材
a **slice** of bread 一片麵包	a **sheet** of zinc 一片鋅	a **roll** of paper 一捲紙
a **bottle** of milk 一瓶牛奶	a **packet** of salt 一小袋鹽	a **sack** of coal 一袋煤炭
a **ball** of yarn 一球紗線	a **pail** of water 一桶水	a **spool** of thread 一軸線
a **speck** of dust 一點灰塵	a **coil** of rope 一捲繩索	

(d) 不可數名詞搭配單數動詞。

USAGE PRACTICE

▶ **Food** is scarce in many developing countries. 許多開發中國家缺乏食物。

▶ The **laughter** of the boys was distinctly clear. 男孩們的笑聲清晰響亮。

▶ **Milk** contains all the necessary nutritious elements. 牛奶含有所有必需的營養成分。

▶ Some **sugar** has been added to sweeten it. 加了一些糖使它甜一點。

▶ **Air** is a mixture of gases. 空氣是多種氣體的混合物。

▶ **Wood** is useful for many purposes. 木材有許多用途。

▶ **Swimming** is a good exercise. 游泳是很好的運動。

▶ The **information** you gave me is not enough. 你給我的訊息不夠充足。

 單數可數名詞也搭配單數動詞。

▶ The **customer** has come to pay you. 那個顧客已經來付你錢了。
▶ A **man** who calls himself Mr. Harper is here to see you. 一個自稱是哈波先生的人來這要見你。

(e) 有些不可數名詞字尾雖是 s，但其後還是接單數動詞。

USAGE PRACTICE

▶ **Economics** was one of the subjects he took. 經濟學是他修的科目之一。

▶ **Rickets** is caused by malnutrition. 營養不良會造成軟骨症。

▶ There has been no **news** about it yet. 至今還然沒有它的相關消息。

(f) 有些名詞表示某一意義時，有可數用法；但是，表示其他意義時，則為不可數用法。

USAGE PRACTICE

▶ How fast time seems to fly. 時光（不可數）飛逝得多快啊。

▶ How many times have you seen that film? 你看過那部影片幾次（可數）了？

▶ A glass is made of glass. 玻璃杯（可數）是用玻璃（不可數）製成的。

▶ Nero was notorious for his cruelty. He inflicted terrible cruelties on his prisoners.
尼祿的殘酷（不可數）惡名昭彰。他在囚犯身上施以殘酷的行為（可數）。

▶ Mr. York is famous for his kindness. He is thanked for his many kindnesses.
約克先生以仁慈（不可數）著名。他因為許多善行（可數）而被感激。

小練習

請依字彙可數或不可數的性質，將其代號填入下方的欄位中。

1. chair
2. cheese
3. mosquito
4. bottle
5. water
6. herd
7. calendar
8. food
9. apple
10. beef
11. oil
12. laughter
13. circus
14. axe
15. envelope
16. paper
17. soap
18. milk
19. hour
20. sunshine
21. example
22. influenza
23. person
24. people
25. dollar
26. money
27. air
28. mud

可數	不可數

☞ 更多相關習題請見本章應用練習 Part 19～Part 21。

2-5 集合名詞

(a) 集合名詞代表一群人、動物或事物。

USAGE PRACTICE

a **bunch** of flowers 一束花

the **staff** of a school 學校全體教職員

a **gang** of robbers 一幫強盜

the **audience** at a concert 一場音樂會的聽眾

an **army** of ants 一大群螞蟻

a **list** of names 一份名單

a **school** of whales 一群鯨魚

a **pack** of dogs 一群狗

a **choir** of singers 一隊合唱團

a **crew** of sailors 一組船員

a **litter** of puppies 一窩小狗

a **troop** of scouts 一隊童子軍

a **range** of mountains 一列山脈

a **herd** of cattle 一群牛

a **crowd** of paparazzi 一群狗仔隊

a **block** of flats 一棟公寓大樓

a **clump** of trees 一叢樹

a **collection** of stamps 一批收藏的郵票

a **panel** of judges 一組裁判

a **fleet** of taxis 一群計程車

(b) 集合名詞當主詞時，若指「整體」時，要搭配單數動詞。

USAGE PRACTICE

▶ The **audience** was delighted with his performance. 觀眾對他的表演感到很開心。

▶ The **band** is playing the national anthem. 這樂隊正在演奏國歌。

▶ The **staff** has donated some money to the orphanage.

全體職員已經捐了一些錢給孤兒院。

▶ A **fleet** of ships was setting out from the harbor. 一個船隊正從港口啟航。

▶ A **list** of names was given to the teacher. 一份名單被交給了老師。

▶ There is a **gang** of thieves operating in that area. 有一夥竊賊在那區域橫行。

▶ A **swarm** of bees lives in that hive. 一大群蜜蜂住在那個蜂巢中。

▶ A **range** of mountains lies to the east of the plain. 有一列山脈橫臥在平原的東方。

▶ A **group** of boys is playing in the garden. 一群男孩正在花園裡遊戲。

▶ There is a **herd** of cattle grazing in the field. 有一群牛在田野吃草。

▶ A **bunch** of bananas does not cost much. 一串香蕉值不了多少錢。

▶ The **committee** wants to withhold the decision. 委員會想要阻擋這個決定。

▶ Our **team** faces strong competition this year. 我們的隊伍今年面臨激烈的競爭。

▶ The **government** is prepared to look into the matter. 政府準備調查此一事件。

(c) 集合名詞當主詞時，若指「團體中的個體們」時，要搭配複數動詞。

USAGE PRACTICE

▶ The **team** are to supply their own rackets. 隊員們要自己準備球拍。

▶ The **gang** are proud of their victories. 這個不良集團對他們的勝利感到自滿。

▶ The **staff** have all gone home by now. 所有工作人員現在都已經回家去了。

▶ The **audience** are clapping their hands. 觀眾們在鼓掌。

▶ The **committee** are divided in their opinions. 委員們意見分歧。

(d) 也有其他的字可以表示「一群為了某特殊目的而聚集的人」。

USAGE PRACTICE

people in a riot 暴動中的人 → **mob** 暴民

people at a service in a church 教堂裡做禮拜的人 → **congregation** （教堂的）會眾

基礎文法寶典 ❶
Essential English Usage & Grammar

| people at a concert/play 欣賞音樂會／戲劇的人 → **audience** 聽眾／觀眾 |
| people at a meeting 參與會議的人 → **assembly** 與會者 |
| people lining up for something 排隊做某事的人 → **line** （人或車的）隊伍 |
| a disorderly crowd 混亂無秩序的人群 → **rabble** 烏合之眾 |
| people of a district 一個地區的人 → **community** 社區 |

請在空格中填入適當的集合名詞。

1. A _____ of judges will decide on the winning entry.

2. Several _____ of flats were built to solve the housing problem.

3. You have to go up a _____ of stairs to reach the bedrooms.

4. An _____ of soldiers marched past the houses.

5. Several pieces of paper fluttered to the floor as a _____ of wind blew through the window.

6. A _____ of people gathered around the scene of the accident. There was a _____ of blood on the road beside the overturned car.

7. The _____ of kittens in the corner were fighting with one another over a reel of thread.

8. Her father owns a _____ of shops and also belongs to the _____ of directors of an insurance company.

9. Looking down through the windows of the plane, we could see a _____ of islands amidst a large expanse of water.

10. The _____ clapped loudly as the _____ of dancers bowed on the stage.

Chapter 2　應用練習

PART 1

請利用 's、' 或 of... 將下列各題改為所有格的型態。

1. the glasses/the frames → _____
2. Mary/desk → _____
3. Charles/dog → _____
4. crocodiles/skins → _____
5. the book/the pages → _____
6. hens/cackling → _____
7. for goodness/sake → _____
8. the dog/barking → _____

9. the sun/rays → _____   10. the flower/the petals → _____

11. the pens/the nibs → _____   12. the kitten/meow → _____

13. the paintings/the colors → _____   14. teachers/meeting → _____

15. old wives/tales → _____   16. children/mother → _____

17. an hour/ride → _____   18. James/notebooks → _____

PART 2

請利用 's、' 或 of... 將下列各題改為所有格的型態。

1. the lioness/cubs → _____   2. the pen/the cover → _____

3. the plant/the flowers → _____   4. Richard/watch → _____

5. the flies/hairy legs → _____   6. no one else/place → _____

7. fifty cents/worth → _____   8. the moon/orbit → _____

9. the tigress/roar → _____   10. corn/the sheaves → _____

11. the train/the coaches → _____   12. Japan/economy → _____

13. yesterday/accident → _____   14. the village fool/antics → _____

15. four months/vacation → _____   16. Great Britain/trade → _____

17. the bottles/the tops → _____   18. China/population → _____

19. an hour/delay → _____   20. for vanity/sake → _____

21. the Coopers/house → _____   22. Napoleon the Third/reign → _____

PART 3

請利用 's、' 或 of... 將下列各題改為所有格的型態。

1. two hours/wait → _____   2. the insect/wings → _____

3. the pencil/the color → _____   4. Russia/policy → _____

5. at my wits/end → _____   6. the tree/the roots → _____

7. the box/the lid → _____   8. a year/work → _____

9. the school/the students → _____   10. the house/the roof → _____

11. the girl/handbag → _____   12. the jungle/the animals → _____

13. the car/the doors → _____   14. out of harm/way → _____

15. the lion/mane → _____   16. Hong Kong/land problem → _____

17. Pluto/diameter → _____   18. the sea/the creatures → _____

基礎文法寶典 ❶
Essential English Usage & Grammar

19. the wind/the force → _____ 20. the bridesmaids/bouquets → _____

21. the cover/the flask → _____ 22. the volcano/the formation → _____

23. the Chief of Police/program → _____ 24. in my mind/eye → _____

PART 4

請在適當位置加上 ' 以形成正確的所有格涵義。

1. Georges mistake
2. Mr. Potters papers
3. the princes horse
4. teachers union
5. my parents idea
6. someone elses money
7. the dogs collar
8. two hours study
9. a weeks holiday
10. the actress jewels
11. the monkeys chatter
12. Mr. James suggestion
13. ten minutes wait
14. the shopkeepers goods
15. the teacher-in-charges help
16. the chief officers pay
17. my sister-in-laws furniture
18. the waitresses attitude

PART 5

請在適當位置加上 ' 或 's，以形成正確且通順的所有格涵義。

1. That is the headmaster office over there.

2. They had a reunion dinner on New Year Eve in Helen house.

3. "One man meat is another man poison," he said.

4. The boys and their dogs ran after Sally cat.

5. The ladies hats were blown away by the wind.

6. The sun rays shone into Agnes room through the window.

7. A week stay with Charles aunt will be enough, I think.

8. I can hear children singing coming from Billy house.

9. "For goodness sake, can't we have an hour peace and quiet in this house?" she asked.

10. Miss Brown car was packed with students from St. Philip Girls School.

11. The naughty child took Elsie books and put them on Jeffrey desk.

12. Mrs. Smith children accidentally sat on an ant nest and were badly bitten.

13. The children have gone to James house with Louise and her sister.

14. "The gentlemen hats are in the master bedroom," the maid said.

15. Many of Lois friends were here yesterday: Peter, Tom, Mary, and even Mary cousin, Paul.

PART 6

請在適當位置加上 ' ' ，以形成正確且通順的所有格涵義。

1. My brothers friends are destroying the wasps nest. They are using the gardeners hose to flood it with water.

2. Her mothers handbag was found in the dogs kennel after three days search.

3. "For Heavens sake, keep quiet. I want to hear Thomas side of the story. I have heard yours."

4. You have to remove the chickens feathers and innards before cooking. The chickens head must be thoroughly cleaned and its claws must be chopped off.

5. My brothers racquets are of the same brand as her brothers.

6. Judy, the butchers daughter, has scored six As in her examination. She is her parents pride and joy.

7. Jeffrey, you should obey your teachers orders. She told you not to write your hs like ls, or your ss like zs.

8. Marys sister is staying at her parents-in-laws house at the moment. She is using her husbands car as he is away.

9. Mans landing on the moon is one of the greatest milestones in history. The two astronauts first steps on the moons surface were witnessed on television by almost everyone.

10. The bridesmaids dresses were lovely, but the brides gown was truly a beautiful creation. A long, flowing veil crowned the brides head.

11. Tell your brothers friend that he must not sit in someone elses place. If I am not mistaken, that is Stephens seat.

12. I can see my uncles car by our gate. He must have come to spend his fortnights vacation with us.

13. "The two dogs barking disturbed the babys sleep. You had better ask the babys mother to come here and rock it to sleep again."

14. At an early age, children are taught the three Rs and to mind their ps and qs when they speak to anyone.

15. I'm going to apply for two weeks leave so that I can stay at my grandfathers farm. His farm is about a days journey by car from here.

16. The witnesses comments were helpful to the policeman. They said that the driver was going at a snails pace when the accident occurred. So he couldn't have caused the accident.

PART 7

請在適當位置加上 ' ，以形成正確且通順的所有格涵義。

1. We shouldn't take a persons things away without asking his or her permission first.

2. This doesn't look like my brothers pen. He must have taken somebody elses by mistake.

3. She has taken a months leave and will be visiting her sisters friends in Newton.

4. The young lawyer did not know what to do. His witness evidence was not sufficient to support his clients case.

5. The suns heat is able to warm the earths surface.

6. The warriors headdresses were brightly-colored.

7. The mechanics jeans are dirty but he doesn't seem to mind.

8. The owls hooting scared the child and made him cry. The childs sister tried to shoo the owl away but it refused to leave its perch.

9. Bettys birthday is just around the corner. With her parents consent, she is having a party at her house.

10. Harriet Beecher Stowe is the author of *Uncle Toms Cabin*. The story is about a black slaves life.

11. The suns rays shone through the foliage, lighting up the path before me. After a moments hesitation, I decided to walk on.

12. My sisters best friends house is just minutes away from ours. They treat each other like sisters and regard each others possessions as their own.

13. She doubted the boys story and accused them of telling lies.

14. After a few days stay at his grandparents house, he decided to come home.

15. That mans sales tactics were very effective. Within a day, he had sold about a hundred thousand dollars worth of insurance policies.

PART 8

請寫出下列字彙的複數形。如果沒有複數形，請打 ✕。

1. cargo _____   2. goose _____   3. fox _____

4. roof _____   5. boot _____   6. fisherman _____

7. passenger _____   8. piano _____   9. mosquito _____

10. mouse _____   11. house _____   12. louse _____

13. bureau _____   14. fungus _____   15. sister-in-law _____

16. grandmother _____   17. passer-by _____   18. larva _____

19. salmon _____   20. armful _____

PART 9

請寫出下列字彙的複數形。如果沒有複數形，請打×。

1. axis _____   2. gallows _____   3. family _____

4. curry _____   5. machinery _____   6. cloth _____

7. chorus _____   8. science _____   9. cactus _____

10. crisis _____   11. medium _____   12. genius _____

13. index _____   14. Monday _____   15. echo _____

PART 10

請將下列句子的粗體部份改為複數形，並進行其他必要的修改，使整個句子正確無誤。

1. The **child** is crying for her mother.

   → _____

2. There is a **mouse** in the kitchen.

   → _____

3. That **truck** is carrying cement to the **factory**.

   → _____

4. **He** knows the name of the **clerk** who works in the office.

   → _____

5. A **life** was lost in the fire last night.

   → _____

6. A **fly** is settling on the food that you have placed on the table.

   → _____

7. There is an easy **way** to do this **sum**.

   → _____

8. The LED **light** on his **bicycle** is not working.

   → _____

9. There is a **farm** at the foot of the **mountain**.

→ _____

10. A **mosquito** is an insect.

    → _____

11. The **flute** is made of bamboo, but the **piano** is not.

    → _____

12. That **volcano** is an active one.

    → _____

13. The **army** retreated, leaving the body of its **hero** behind.

    → _____

PART 11

請將下列句子的粗體部份改為複數形，並進行其他必要的修改，使整個句子正確無誤。

1. The **thief** who snatched the **lady**'s handbag was caught.

    → _____

2. The **woman** was shocked, wasn't she?

    → _____

3. The larva of the **mosquito** comes up to the surface of the water to breathe.

    → _____

4. Is there any **remedy** for this **type** of sickness?

    → _____

5. My **sister-in-law** likes fish.

    → _____

6. The **farmer** was carrying an **armful** of hay into the **barn**.

    → _____

7. The **foreman** ordered the **worker** to report to the **manager**.

    → _____

8. The **doorbell** of that **house** has been out of order since last week, hasn't it?

    → _____

9. **I** measured the radius of the **circle** and wrote the **figure** down in my **notebook**.

    → _____

10. This **phenomenon** can be explained, can't it?

→ _____

11. The **cowherd** was driving the cattle home when he was attacked by a **bandit**.

→ _____

12. The **pupa** changes into a butterfly after a few weeks, doesn't it?

→ _____

13. The **child**'s act amused the audience a great deal.

→ _____

14. The **headman** was very proud of his **son-in-law**.

→ _____

15. **I** discovered that the can **opener** was rusty and that the rust had got into the **can** of milk.

→ _____

PART 12

請將下列句子的粗體部份改為複數形，並進行其他必要的修改，使整個句子正確無誤。

1. The **passer-by** stopped and stared at the crying **child**.

→ _____

2. The **artist** has a **studio** in the **apartment**, doesn't he?

→ _____

3. Does your **car** always have a **breakdown** in the middle of the **road**?

→ _____

4. A **louse** is a small insect living on the **body** of an animal.

→ _____

5. The **cook** was measuring a **cupful** of sugar into the mixing **bowl**.

→ _____

6. On Friday the **gentleman** likes to take a **walk** along the **cliff**.

→ _____

7. The **washerwoman** was hanging up the **shirt** on the **clothes-line**.

→ _____

8. The roof of the mud **house** has a gutter **pipe** to lead the water away when it rains.

→ _____

9. Is the **officer-in-charge** supposed to collect the **report** from the **cadet**?

→ _____

10. There was a traffic **game** in the **playground** for the **child** during Road Safety **Week**.

→ _____

11. There is a large **room** with a French **window** in the **house**.

→ _____

12. The **maid** set a **mousetrap** to catch the **mouse**, but it was clever enough to avoid it.

→ _____

PART 13

請利用提示的字彙，在空格中填入正確的單複數形式。

1. **work**

   I'm not free at the moment; I have some _____ to do.

   Every English scholar shows appreciation for the _____ of Shakespeare.

2. **glass**

   A mirror is made of _____ .

   The pair of _____ on that shelf were cracked.

3. **kindness**

   His _____ were much appreciated by the villagers.

   He contributed a large sum of money out of _____ .

4. **art**

   Those beautiful gardens owe more to _____ than to nature.

   He is well-versed in the fine _____ .

5. **anxiety**

   The new policy removed all _____ about higher income taxes.

   His _____ to please his stepmother touched their hearts.

6. **people**

   The Governor appealed to the _____ to remain calm.

   The United Nations hoped for harmony among the _____ of the world.

7. **cruelty**

   The slaves suffered great _____ under their taskmasters.

   _____ in a person is much detested.

8. **love**

There's no _____ lost between the two brothers.

His _____ include the sciences and the arts.

9. **jealousy**

I'm tired of the _____ and quarrels between the two neighbors.

He showed great _____ of his rival's success.

10. **misery**

He shot the dog to put it out of its _____ .

The _____ of mankind have been with us since time immemorial.

PART 14

請寫出下列字彙的名詞。

1. pure _____
2. clean _____
3. judge _____
4. efficient _____
5. speak _____
6. clever _____
7. simple _____
8. accurate _____
9. oppose _____
10. reduce _____
11. explain _____
12. punctual _____
13. marry _____
14. vacant _____
15. apply _____
16. ugly _____
17. believe _____
18. breathe _____
19. criticize _____
20. rely _____
21. depend _____
22. conduct _____
23. moist _____
24. succeed _____

PART 15

請寫出下列字彙的名詞。

1. allocate _____
2. omit _____
3. choose _____
4. analyze _____
5. prophet _____
6. obey _____
7. divide _____
8. live _____
9. deny _____
10. die _____
11. personify _____
12. hate _____
13. splendid _____
14. exceed _____
15. short _____
16. receive _____

PART 16

請依提示在空格中填入正確的名詞。務必注意該字彙的單複數形式。

1. _____ (**know**) is a treasure, but _____ (**practice**) is the key to it.

2. The _____ (**irregular**) of her _____ (**attend**) at school made her teacher suspicious.

3. "Don't let your _____ (**imagine**) run wild," he told her.

4. _____ (**succeed**) went to his head and he began to treat his friends with _____ (**contemptuous**).

5. The doctors were pleased with the quick _____ (**recover**) of the patient. The _____ (**effective**) of the drug was clearly evident.

6. With the _____ (**arrive**) of the baby, her _____ (**happy**) was complete.

7. In _____ (**frustrate**) he threw away the jar; its _____ (**content**) spilled all over the path.

8. In _____ (**recognize**) of his brave _____ (**do**), he was decorated with the Victoria Cross.

9. In his _____ (**speak**), the headmaster emphasized the _____ (**necessary**) for students to do well in the _____ (**examine**).

10. "In this world, there is no _____ (**just**) or _____ (**equal**)," he said bitterly.

11. The _____ (**promote**) of _____ (**tour**) is the main _____ (**concerned**) of the board.

12. We had to pass an _____ (**intelligent**) test before we could gain _____ (**admit**) to the organization.

13. The _____ (**believe**) is that anyone who bathes in the pond will have everlasting _____ (**young**) and _____ (**beautiful**).

14. His heart was torn between _____ (**loyal**) to his country and _____ (**devote**) to his mother.

15. I did not have much _____ (**choose**), so I signed the _____ (**agree**).

16. The _____ (**die**) of the old chief caused great _____ (**grieve**) to the villagers. They gave him a grand _____ (**bury**).

17. You must remember that we have to pay for the _____ (**wrap**) and the _____ (**ship**) of the goods.

18. I have some _____ (**write**) that requires your _____ (**assist**).

PART 17

請依提示在空格中填入正確的名詞。務必注意該字彙的單複數形式。

1. She was full of _____ (**angry**) at the cruel _____ (**treat**) of these _____ (**prison**).

2. After she had done her _____ (**work**) to her _____ (**satisfy**), she went to the factory to see how the _____ (**produce**) of _____ (**good**) was going on.

3. His _____ (**believe**) is that no one can pass _____ (**judge**) on another. All _____ (**man**) are equal in his sight and all _____ (**man**) can err.

4. With the _____ (**except**) of Joe, all the students were present. The _____ (**teach**) hoped that Joe would make an _____ (**appear**) soon.

5. This is an exercise on the _____ (**pronounce**) of words. See that the students put _____ (**emphasize**) on the syllables underlined.

6. As soon as we heard the _____ (**announce**), we demanded an _____ (**explain**) from the _____ (**manage**).

7. For the _____ (**safe**) of the _____ (**refuge**), the _____ (**govern**) has established a new _____ (**settle**) away from the border.

8. His _____ (**confess**) that he was indeed the _____ (**murder**) that the police were looking for was a _____ (**reveal**) to us since we had no _____ (**suspect**) at all.

9. There are no _____ (**occupy**) in that house. If you want to make an _____ (**inspect**) of the grounds, you'll have to obtain _____ (**permit**) from the agents.

10. At the _____ (**conclude**) of the _____ (**meet**), the president made an _____ (**announce**) about his _____ (**resign**).

11. The _____ (**invade**) of the island by the _____ (**foreign**) caused _____ (**confuse**) among the _____ (**inhabit**).

12. In their _____ (**defend**) of the fort, they made a _____ (**select**) of a hundred men known for their _____ (**strong**) and _____ (**valiant**) to guard the gates.

13. How the _____ (**create**) of man came about is a _____ (**mysterious**) that has no _____ (**solve**).

14. The _____ (**simple**) and _____ (**innocent**) of children may vanish when they reach _____ (**adult**) and come face-to-face with _____ (**real**).

15. His _____ (**suggest**) that there should be a _____ (**reduce**) in the wages for the

_____ (**work**) was shouted down by the assembly.

16. From the _____ (**express**) on her face and her nervous _____ (**move**), I could see that she was filled with _____ (**anxious**) over the _____ (**lose**) of the money.

PART 18

請依提示在空格中填入正確的名詞。務必注意該字彙的單複數形式。

1. The _____ (**destroy**) caused by the fire was widespread. Fortunately, the _____ (**major**) of the houses were covered by _____ (**insure**), while the remaining few were still under _____ (**construct**).

2. Mathematics is an interesting subject. The simple rule of _____ (**add**), _____ (**subtract**), _____ (**multiply**), and _____ (**divide**) are taught at an early age.

3. Did you meet with any _____ (**oppose**) at the meeting? Was the Board of Directors angry at your numerous _____ (**suggest**) ?

4. Too much _____ (**expose**) to the sun is not good for health.

5. The sea has given _____ (**inspire**) to many poets and _____ (**art**).

6. Despite the doctor's _____ (**reassure**), the patient's condition became worse.

7. The _____ (**rival**) between the two top students in the school is very keen, and so is the _____ (**compete**) among the rest of the students.

8. She is often praised for her _____ (**efficient**) in her work and has been recommended for _____ (**promote**).

9. What is the _____ (**weigh**) of this sack of potatoes?

10. Heroes are always rewarded for their acts of _____ (**brave**) and courage.

11. The criminals were put on _____ (**try**) and later given a sentence of capital _____ (**punish**).

12. The _____ (**coward**) of a bully is often looked upon with disgust.

13. A piece of _____ (**advise**) that most teachers give to their students is that they should look up their own _____ (**refer**) on subjects that they don't know much about.

14. It is an _____ (**offend**) to show disrespect to any panel of judges.

PART 19

請在空格中正確填入 much、many、a few、a little 或 any 等字彙。

1. She made so _____ promises, but she never kept _____ of them.

2. Didn't you ask him how _____ the tickets cost?

3. "How _____ students were in the library this afternoon?" "There were only _____."

4. Not _____ of the girls in our school took part in the fashion parade.

5. Put _____ salt into the soup. Don't put too _____ into it.

6. We haven't got _____ time left. Let's not take _____ of the luggage with us. We can come back for it later on.

7. The restaurant is just _____ blocks away. I don't have _____ money, but just enough for dinner.

8. There isn't _____ petrol in the tank. The car will not go for more than _____ kilometers.

9. "How _____ do you know about his plans for further study abroad?" "I know only _____ about them."

10. Not _____ of us know how to write French. Only _____ of us have studied the language.

11. Is there _____ milk in the refrigerator? We need _____ to bake a cake.

12. Don't ask _____ of your brothers to do the exercises for you. You must try _____ on your own at least.

13. How _____ of the boys went to the exhibition yesterday? I met _____ of them in town.

14. I haven't got _____ rice in the house. Please go out to buy _____ kilograms from the shop nearby.

15. There aren't _____ ripe lemons on the tree, but you may pick _____ if you like.

PART 20

請選擇正確的用法填入空格中。

1. The child _____ (*has, have*) been asking for _____ (*his, their*) mother.

2. All the questions _____ (*was, were*) easy, and I managed to answer them within a short time.

3. Her weight _____ (*has, have*) been going down for the past few months.

4. Their laughter _____ (*is, are*) so loud that I can't concentrate on my work.

5. The disease _____ (*has, have*) spread throughout the city, and many people _____ (*is, are*) falling ill.

6. Do you _____ (*think, thinks*) that the milk _____ (*has, have*) turned sour?

7. There _____ (*is, are*) only a little food left. Most of it _____ (*has, have*) been eaten already.

8. All the sheep _____ (*was, were*) wandering all over the road, and _____ (*it, they*) held up the traffic.

9. The traffic _____ (*has, have*) slowed down, and the cars _____ (*is, are*) moving slowly.

10. When the floodwaters _____ (*has, have*) gone down, we will have to rebuild our house.

11. There _____ (*is, are*) two jugs of milk in the refrigerator. One of them _____ (*is, are*) for you.

12. Her efforts _____ (*has, have*) been wasted. Her grades _____ (*is, are*) the lowest in the class.

13. He told me that there _____ (*was, were*) many people coming, but there _____ (*wasn't, weren't*) enough space for all.

14. There _____ (*is, are*) only a little water in the jug bottle. Most of it _____ (*has, have*) evaporated.

15. There _____ (*isn't, aren't*) much money left. So there _____ (*is, are*) going to be some changes in the budget. Refreshments _____ (*is, are*) going to be cut down; so _____ (*is, are*) traveling expenses.

PART 21

請選擇正確的用法填入空格中。

1. We did not see _____ (*many, much*) friends at the party.

2. One of the beggars, who _____ (*was, were*) blind, _____ (*has, have*) been killed in an accident.

3. _____ (*Many, Much*) members of the society _____ (*is, are*) dissatisfied with the rules.

4. Curious things _____ (*has, have*) been happening in that house, which _____ (*was, were*) damaged during the war.

5. There _____ (*is, are*) only _____ (*a little, a few*) space in this shelf for the books. Find _____ (*some, any*) other place to keep them.

6. There _____ (*was, were*) not _____ (*many, much*) damage caused by the floods, which _____ (*was, were*) not as bad as _____ (*that, those*) of last year.

7. There _____ (*isn't, aren't*) _____ (*many, any, much*) biscuits left. I gave the last one to the child who _____ (*was, were*) here yesterday.

8. _____ (*A large number, A large amount*) of the food _____ (*has, have*) gone bad, so we will have to throw all of _____ (*it, them*) away.

9. There _____ (*isn't, aren't*) _____ (*many, much*) we _____ (*has, have*) to do here. The only thing _____ (*is, are*) to trim the hedges.

10. The hunter _____ (*was, were*) fortunate and did not find _____ (*much, many*) difficulty in tracking down the tiger. The only difficulty _____ (*was, were*) in making as _____ (*few, little*) noise as possible.

PART 22

請選擇正確的用法填入空格中。

1. _____ (*Many, Much*) members of the club _____ (*is, are*) thinking of resigning.

2. _____ (*A large amount, A great number*) of money _____ (*is, are*) needed to get this business started.

3. There _____ (*wasn't, weren't*) _____ (*many, much*) good books to choose from, so we bought only _____ (*a few, a little*).

4. A _____ (*flock, brood*) of birds _____ (*was, were*) seen flying south to warmer lands.

5. _____ (*A few, A little*) of that acid _____ (*is, are*) added to the mixture to coagulate it.

6. Their _____ (*team, gang*) of players _____ (*was, were*) no match for our team.

7. _____ (*A great number, A great amount*) of the students _____ (*has, have*) obtained higher grades.

8. _____ (*Was, Were*) there _____ (*a lot, a great deal*) of spectators at the game?

9. There _____ (*isn't, aren't*) _____ (*many, much*) work to be done now, so you can go home.

10. A _____ (nest, swarm) of mice _____ (was, were) found hidden beneath the floor-boards.

11. _____ (A group, A crew) of villagers _____ (has, have) been badly frightened by the tiger.

12. There _____ (wasn't, weren't) _____ (many, much) trouble in finding the new apartment.

13. The _____ (troop, team) of soldiers _____ (has, have) had _____ (a great number, a great deal) of experience in jungle warfare.

14. _____ (A cluster, A bunch) of bananas _____ (cost, costs) only _____ (a little, a few) cents in the village.

15. _____ (A lot, A number) of effort _____ (has, have) been put into the research, and the results _____ (is, are) beyond their expectations.

16. _____ (A few, A great deal of) dust _____ (has, have) settled on the furniture since we last cleaned it.

17. _____ (Was, Were) there _____ (a little, a lot of) mistakes in their essays?

18. _____ (A large amount, A great number) of sugar _____ (was, were) stored in the warehouse.

Chapter 3 代名詞

3-1 人稱代名詞

	主 格	受 格
第一人稱單數（我）	I	me
第一人稱複數（我們）	we	us
第二人稱單數（你）	you	you
第二人稱複數（你們）	you	you
第三人稱單數（他）	he	him
（她）	she	her
（它／牠）	it	it
第三人稱複數（他們、她們、它／牠們）	they	them

(a) 人稱代名詞可以當主詞（使用主格）。

USAGE PRACTICE

▶ **I** can do it. 我會做這事。

▶ **I** am going to school. 我正要去學校。

▶ **You** stand there. 你站在那裡。

▶ **He** scored a goal. 他進球得分。

▶ **He** ran down the hill. 他跑下山丘。

▶ **She** painted it. 她畫它。

▶ **It** dropped on the floor. 它掉在地板上。

▶ **It** gave birth to five kittens last week. 牠上個星期生了五隻小貓。

▶ **We** paid the boy. 我們付了錢給這男孩。

▶ **We** bought a new car last month. 我們上個月買了一部新車。

▶ **You** will both pass. 你們兩個都會通過。

▶ **They** found the treasure. 他們發現了這個寶藏。

▶ **They** went home. 他們回家去了。

▶ **I** am not feeling well. 我不太舒服。

▶ **I** am right. 我是對的。

▶ **You** will do it. 你將會做這事。

▶ **He** was happy. 他很快樂。

▶ **He** speaks English. 他說英文。

▶ **She** likes it. 她喜歡它。

▶ **We** will come. 我們將會來。

▶ Will **you** all be there? 你們都會在那裡嗎？

▶ **They** are helpful. 它們很有幫助。

(b) 人稱代名詞可以當動詞的受詞（使用受格）。

▶ No one saw **me**. 沒有人看到我。　▶ Let **me** go, please! 請讓我走吧！

▶ They have chosen **me**. 他們已經選了我。　▶ Mary will show **you**. 瑪麗將會拿給你看。

▶ I like **you**. 我喜歡你。　▶ They want **you**. 他們需要你。

▶ I will let **you** and **him** go. 我會讓你和他走。

▶ Don't let **him** bully **you**! 別讓他欺侮你！　▶ Mrs. Brown called **him**. 布朗太太叫他。

▶ She recognized **him** at once. 她立刻認出他。

▶ We took **him** to the doctor. 我們帶他去就醫。

▶ Let **him** decide for himself. 讓他自己決定。

▶ Mr. Johnson taught **him**. 強森先生教他。　▶ Let **her** come in. 讓她進來吧。

▶ I took **her** to the movies. 我帶她去看電影。

▶ Who borrowed **it**? 誰把它借走了？　▶ Someone picked **it** up. 有人把它撿起來。

▶ Call **him/her/it** here. 叫他／她／牠過來這裡。

▶ It took **us** a long time to carry **it** down. 我們花了很多時間才把它搬下來。

▶ Mary told **us**. 瑪麗告訴我們。　▶ He helped **us**. 他幫助我們。

▶ Did anyone hear **them**? 有人聽到他們嗎？　▶ She asked **them**. 她問他們。

▶ He rewarded **them**. 他酬謝他們。

▶ I found **them** in the garden. 我在花園找到他們。

▶ Let **them** do as they like. 讓他們照喜歡的方式去做吧。

(c) 人稱代名詞可以當介系詞的受詞（使用受格）。

▶ He gave it to **me**. 他把它給我。　▶ He called for **me**. 他來接我。

▶ He handed the book to **me**. 他把書遞給我。

▶ The teacher will give them to **you**. 老師會把它們給你。

▶ Why is there always an argument between **you** and **them**? 為何你和他們總在爭論？

▶ Between **you** and **me**, I think that we will win the match.

這是你我之間的祕密，我想我們會贏得比賽。

▶ The lady hold hands with **him**. 這位女士和他牽著手。

▶ He took the bag along with **him**. 他隨身帶著那個手提袋。

▶ I'd rather sit between **you** and **him**. 我情願坐在你和他中間。

▶ I laughed at **her**. 我嘲笑她。　　　▶ It was given to **her**. 這東西給了她。

▶ Many people talked about **her**. 許多人談論她。

▶ Is there much difference between **her** and **me**? 她和我之間有很大的差異嗎？

▶ He sat between **her** and **me** at the concert. 在音樂會中，他坐在她和我之間。

▶ They shook hands with **us**. 他們和我們握手。

▶ That man pointed to **us**. 那個男人指著我們。

(d) 在現今的用法中，be 動詞後的代名詞習慣用受格，而不用主格。

USAGE PRACTICE

▶ "Who's there?" "It's **me**!" 「是誰在那裡？」「是我！」

▶ I think it was **him**, not **her**. 我認為那是他，而不是她。

▶ That's **him** standing there. 站在那裡的是他。

▶ If I were **her**, I wouldn't go. 如果我是她，我就不會去。

▶ Don't be alarmed; it's only **us**. 別驚慌，只不過是我們罷了。

▶ It is **us** you saw on the train, not **them**. 你在火車上看到的是我們，而不是他們。

▶ Is that **them** in the photograph? 在照片中的是他們嗎？

 但是在關係子句中，先行詞若是 be 動詞後的代名詞，要視其所扮演的角色來決定要用主格或受格；換言之，先行詞若在子句中作主詞，代名詞要用主格；先行詞若在子句中作受詞，代名詞要用受格。

▶ It is **I** who will get the blame. 是我會被責備。　▶ It was **they** who took it. 是他們拿走它的。

▶ It's **he** who played the record just now. 剛才是他在放唱片。

▶ It was **he** who did the work. 是他做這工作的。

▶ It's **us** whom they should blame. 他們應該責備的是我們。

(e) 在 than 和 as 之後的代名詞，可視其在子句中所扮演的角色，來決定要使用主格或受格。

USAGE PRACTICE

▶ I know you better than **she** (does). 我比她更了解你。

▶ I know you better than (I know) **her**. 我了解你比了解她更多。

▶ I helped you more than **she** (does). 我幫你比她幫你來得多。

▶ You like her as much as **he** (does). 你和他一樣喜歡她。

▶ You like her as much as (you like) **him**. 你一樣喜歡她和他。

 但是在現代用法中，有一律使用受格的趨勢。而如果意思上可能會混淆時，則把原先省略的部分恢復。

▶ She is as tall as **me**. 她和我一樣高。　　▶ She is better than **him**. 她比他好。

▶ He does it as well as **them**. 他做得和他們一樣好。

▶ Carlos did this better than **he did them**. 卡洛斯做這個比做它們（其他事）好。

(f) 和其他人稱一起使用時，第一人稱代名詞 (I、we、me、us) 總是置於其他人稱之後。

USAGE PRACTICE

▶ My sister and **I** are going to town. 我妹妹和我要去鎮上。

▶ Eddie, Ben, Peter, and **I** will help arrange the chairs.

艾迪、班、彼得和我將協助安排座位。

▶ She praised Eliza, Lucy, and **me**. 她稱讚了伊莉莎、露西和我。

▶ He called Jane, Robin, and **me** to his office. 他把珍、羅賓和我叫到他的辦公室。

▶ The match was between those schoolboys and **us**. 這是那些男學童和我們之間的比賽。

(g) 當兩個子句的主詞為相同的代名詞，並用對等連接詞加以連接時，第二個子句主詞可以省略。

USAGE PRACTICE

▶ She sat down and (she) began to work. 她坐下來開始工作。

▶ He has finished his work and (he has) gone home. 他已經完成他的工作，然後回家了。

▶ I fell down but (I) did not cry. 我跌倒了，但是沒哭。

(h) 對於不知道性別的嬰兒、動物，或是沒有性別之分的車輛、船隻，通常用代名詞 it 來表示。

▶ Look at this baby. **It** is so cute! 看看這個小嬰兒。它好可愛啊！

▶ In that baby carriage, there's a baby and **it**'s crying. 那嬰兒車裡有個嬰兒，它正在哭。

▶ The ship has left the harbor. **It** is sailing for Tasmania.

船已經離港了。它正駛往塔斯馬尼亞島。

▶ He bought a new car and **it** cost him ten thousand dollars. 他買了新車，花了一萬美金。

I work on this ship. Isn't **she** a beauty? 我在這艘船上工作。她是不是很美麗？

★交通工具例如車、船、飛機等，有時候會以 she 稱呼來表示情感。

(i) 傳統上，代名詞 he 可以用來代替中性名詞。當不確定性別時，常假定其為男性。

▶ A teacher has a lot of work to do. **He** has little leisure time.

老師有許多工作要做。很少有休閒時間。

▶ A doctor is responsible for the health of **his** patients. 醫師要對病人的健康負責。

▶ Anyone can pass if **he** tries. 只要嘗試，任何人都能通過。

▶ Each must do what **he** can. 每個人都必須盡其所能。

▶ Everybody should be satisfied with what **he** has. 每個人都應該滿足現狀。

注意 但是現在由於女男平權的意識抬頭，常會寫成 "he/she" 或 "he or she"。

▶ A student will definitely be failed if **he/she** is caught cheating.
學生如果被抓到作弊，一定會被評為不及格。

▶ Anyone can succeed if **he or she** wants to. 任何人如果有意願，都可能成功。

(j) 在附加問句中，要用複數人稱代名詞來代替 everybody/everyone、somebody/someone、anybody/anyone 或 nobody/no one 等不定代名詞。

▶ <u>Everybody</u> is ready, aren't **they**? 每個人都準備好了，不是嗎？

▶ Not <u>anybody</u> can do it, can **they**? 不是任何人都會做，是吧？

▶ <u>Someone</u> has been smoking in here, haven't **they**? 有人在這裡抽過煙，不是嗎？

▶ Somebody took it by mistake, didn't **they**? 有人誤拿走了它，不是嗎？

▶ Nobody has seen it yet, have **they**? 沒有人看過它，對吧？

小練習

寫出下列名詞的正確人稱代名詞用字，包括主格與受格。

1. the telephone → _____ → _____
2. the children → _____ → _____
3. the actors → _____ → _____
4. the sad news → _____ → _____
5. the results → _____ → _____
6. the trees → _____ → _____
7. dance → _____ → _____
8. Tom and I → _____ → _____
9. you and Lionel → _____ → _____
10. her aunt → _____ → _____
11. Mr. and Mrs. Smith → _____ → _____
12. our bags → _____ → _____
13. my father → _____ → _____
14. the headmaster → _____ → _____
15. both men → _____ → _____
16. the captain of the team → _____ → _____
17. those stories → _____ → _____
18. two spoonfuls of sugar → _____ → _____
19. his nephew → _____ → _____
20. a liter of milk → _____ → _____

☞ 更多相關習題請見本章應用練習 Part 1～Part 7。

3-2 所有格代名詞

	人稱代名詞	所有格	所有格代名詞
第一人稱單數（我）	I	my	mine
第一人稱複數（我們）	we	our	ours
第二人稱單數（你）	you	your	yours
第二人稱複數（你們）	you	your	yours
第三人稱單數（他）	he	his	his
（她）	she	her	hers
（它／牠）	it	its	its
第三人稱複數（他們、她們、它／牠們）	they	their	theirs

(a) 所有格代名詞相當於「所有格 + 名詞」。所有格代名詞後面不接名詞。

所有格 + 名詞	所有格代名詞
▶ This is <u>my room</u>. 這是我的房間。	→ This is **mine**. 這是我的（房間）。
▶ That is <u>my pen</u>. 那是我的筆。	→ That is **mine**. 那是我的（筆）。
▶ This is <u>your dog</u>. 這是你的狗。	→ This is **yours**. 這是你的（狗）。
▶ It is <u>his ring</u>. 這是他的戒指。	→ It is **his**. 這是他的（戒指）。
▶ It is <u>his desk</u>. 這是他的桌子。	→ It is **his**. 這是他的（桌子）。
▶ It is <u>her thermos bottle</u>. 這是她的熱水瓶。	→ It is **hers**. 這是她的（熱水瓶）。
▶ They are <u>her dresses</u>. 它們是她的衣服。	→ They are **hers**. 它們是她的（衣服）。
▶ That is <u>our car</u>. 那是我們的車。	→ That is **ours**. 那是我們的（車）。
▶ These are <u>our books</u>. 這些是我們的書。	→ These are **ours**. 這些是我們的（書）。
▶ That is <u>their camera</u>. 那是他們的照相機。	→ That is **theirs**. 那是他們的（照相機）。
▶ That is <u>their car</u>. 那是他們的車子。	→ That is **theirs**. 那是他們的（車）。

▶ Those are my shoes. They are **mine**. 那些是我的鞋子，它們是我的。

▶ This is my bag. It is **mine**. 這是我的袋子，它是我的。

▶ Your car and **mine** are of the same make. 你的車和我的是同一個廠牌。

▶ These are my books. **Yours** are over there. 這些是我的書，你的在那邊。

▶ "Are these his shirts?" "Yes, they are **his**." 「這些是他的襯衫嗎？」「是的，它們是他的。」

▶ This pen is **hers** and that one is **his**. 這枝筆是她的，那枝是他的。

▶ These are not our books; those are **ours**. 這些不是我們的書；那些才是我們的。

▶ Their house is much smaller than **ours**. 他們的房子比我們的小多了。

▶ These cards are **ours**; **theirs** are over there. 這些卡片是我們的，他們的在那裡。

▶ Our cat and **theirs** are playing in the garden. 我們的貓和他們的貓正在花園裡玩。

 不論是口語或閱讀，一般都很少使用所有格代名詞 its，因為很不自然。

▶ This is a <u>rat's nest</u>. 這是一隻老鼠的巢。(ˣThis nest is **its**.)

(b) 所有格代名詞可以單獨使用，其後不加所有格符號。

USAGE PRACTICE

▶ Those comics are **ours**. 那些漫畫書是我們的。(不可寫成 ours')

▶ This house is **hers**. 這房子是她的。(不可寫成 hers')

▶ Is this **yours**? 這是你的嗎?(不可寫成 yours')

▶ **Ours** are here; **theirs** are over there.

我們的東西在這裡,他們的東西在那裡。(不可寫成 ours'、theirs')

▶ He has borrowed **hers**, not **yours**.

他已經借了她的東西,不是你的。(不可寫成 hers'、yours')

(c) 「of + 所有格代名詞」是雙重所有格,其意為「…中的一個」。

USAGE PRACTICE

▶ The boy is a friend **of mine**. 這男孩是我的一個朋友。

▶ A friend **of mine** has invited me to his birthday party.

我的一個朋友已邀請我去參加他的生日派對。

▶ Can I borrow a pencil **of yours**? 我可以借用你的一枝鉛筆嗎?

▶ Is that girl a cousin **of yours**? 那女孩是你的一個堂妹嗎?

▶ He gave it to a cousin **of his**. 他把它給了他的一個表弟。

▶ It was through no fault **of his** that the accident occurred. 那件意外的發生並非他的錯。

▶ An uncle **of ours** is coming here during the weekend. 我們的一個叔叔週末要來這裡。

▶ Is she a relative **of theirs**? 她是他們的一個親戚嗎?

▶ They met an old friend **of theirs**. 他們遇見他們的一個老朋友。

(d) 所有格代名詞當主詞時,必須注意搭配正確的單數或複數動詞。

USAGE PRACTICE

▶ Your pen is cheap, but **mine** is expensive. 你的筆很便宜,但我的很貴。

(mine 相當於 my pen,接單數動詞 is)

▶ My pencil is sharp, but **yours** is blunt. 我的鉛筆很尖,但你的很鈍。

(yours 相當於 your pencil,接單數動詞 is)

▶ My shoes are clean; **yours** are dirty. 我的鞋子很乾淨,你的很髒。

(yours 相當於 your shoes,接複數動詞 are)

▶ Your shirts are here, and **his** are over there. 你的襯衫在這裡,他的在那裡。

（his 相當於 his shirts，接複數動詞 are）

▶ My room is clean, but **hers** is cleaner. 我的房間很乾淨，但是她的更乾淨。

（hers 相當於 her room，接單數動詞 is）

▶ Their books are marked, but **ours** are not. 他們的書被做記號了，但是我們的沒有。

（ours 相當於 our books，接複數動詞 are）

 小練習

請用正確的所有格代名詞來取代下列句子中的粗體部分。

1. Please ask him to send in **his application** early. You must not forget to send in **your application**, either. _____ _____

2. **Her painting** is very good but **your painting** is even better. _____ _____

3. Those are **my handkerchiefs;** they can't be **her handkerchiefs.** _____ _____

4. We can manage with **our work.** Can you and your friends manage with **your work**?
_____ _____

5. They exchanged **their books** for **our books** yesterday. _____ _____

6. I saw a brother of **Mary's** the other day. He was having his lunch and I was having **my lunch** at a restaurant. _____ _____

7. Two sons of **Mr. and Mrs. Bright's** are studying at the university at present. _____

8. I wonder if I can borrow **Nancy's dictionary**. I have lent her **my dictionary** several times.
_____ _____

9. **Our hockey sticks** have got mixed up with **their hockey sticks**. _____ _____

10. I'm not sure whether I wrote **my name** on the test paper. Did you write **your name**?
_____ _____

11. **Peter's watch** is not showing the correct time but **my sister's watch** is.
_____ _____

12. Our room is always clean and tidy, while **Alex and Jim's room** is the opposite of **our room.**
_____ _____

13. **David's bicycle** is here, and so is **your bicycle.** Where is **Peggy's bicycle**?
_____ _____ _____

14. If you are interested in butterflies, you should look at Philip's collection. **His collection** is the

largest that I have ever seen; it even beats **my collection**. _____ _____

15. My brother's fishing rod is broken, so I cannot use **his fishing rod**. I'll have to borrow **your fishing rod**. _____ _____

16. We can get **our car** out of the parking lot, but I don't think that you can do the same thing with **your car**. _____ _____

17. He did not see **Victor's bag and my bag** beside the chairs; that's why he sat down there.

_____

18. They will have to arrange **their books** on the table and Gary has to put **his books** on the shelf.

_____ _____

☞ 更多相關習題請見本章應用練習 Part 8～Part 11。

3-3 反身代名詞

	人稱代名詞	反身代名詞
第一人稱單數（我）	I	myself
第一人稱複數（我們）	we	ourselves
第二人稱單數（你）	you	yourself
第二人稱複數（你們）	you	yourselves
第三人稱單數（他）	he	himself
（她）	she	herself
（它／牠）	it	itself
第三人稱複數（他們、她們、它／牠們）	they	themselves

(a) 反身代名詞可直接當及物動詞的受詞，表示主詞與受詞是同一人。

USAGE PRACTICE

▶ I told **myself** not to be frightened. 我告訴自己不要害怕。

▶ I hurt **myself**. 我傷了自己。

▶ I behaved **myself** very well. 我表現良好。

▶ I made **myself** a birthday cake. 我為自己做了生日蛋糕。

▶ You should ask **yourself** to practice more. 你應該要求自己勤加練習。

▶ He hit **himself** accidentally. 他不小心擊中自己。

▶ He taught **himself** how to swim. 他無師自通學會游泳。

▶ He pinched **himself** to see if he was dreaming. 他捏自己看是否在做夢。

▶ She told **herself** that she must be brave. 她告訴自己她一定要勇敢。

▶ She cut **herself** when she was peeling the apple. 削蘋果皮時，她割傷了自己。

▶ She sewed **herself** a dress. 她為自己縫製了一件洋裝。

▶ It scratched **itself**. 牠給自己抓癢。

▶ The dog licked **itself** after the fight. 打架後，這隻狗舔舔自己。

▶ We enjoyed **ourselves**. 我們玩得很愉快。

▶ We blame **ourselves** for being stubborn. 我們因頑固而自責。

▶ We made **ourselves** some lemonade. 我們為自己做了一些檸檬水。

▶ They lost **themselves** on the way home. 他們在回家途中迷路了。

▶ They could blame only **themselves** for the accident. 發生這樣的意外，他們只能怪自己。

▶ They made **themselves** a tent. 他們為自己做了一個帳篷。

(b) 反身代名詞也可以當介系詞的受詞。

USAGE PRACTICE

▶ I looked closely at **myself** in the mirror. 我仔細看鏡子中的自己。

▶ I was grumbling to **myself**. 我對自己發牢騷。

▶ You were muttering to **yourself** just now. 你剛才一個人喃喃自語。

▶ Order it for **yourself**, Mary. 瑪麗，妳自己點餐。

▶ You must look after **yourselves**. 你們必須照顧自己。

▶ He cut a slice of cake for **himself**. 他為自己切了一片蛋糕。

▶ She put aside some money for **herself**. 她為她自己存了一些錢。

▶ We are not worried about **ourselves**, but we still have to think of him.

我們並不擔心我們自己，但還是必須考慮到他。

▶ They see only good in **themselves**. 他們只看到自己的優點。

▶ They were talking about **themselves**. 他們在談論自己的事。

▶ They made the cupboard all by **themselves**. 他們全靠自己做了一個餐具櫥。

(c) 反身代名詞可以用來加強語氣，當作名詞或代名詞的同位語，用來加強其重要性，通常放在其所強調的字後面或句尾。

▶ I **myself** found it difficult to do. 我自己發現它很難做。

▶ I lent it to him **myself**. 我自己把它借給了他。

▶ You **yourself** should know what to do. 你自己應該知道該做什麼事。

▶ You **yourself** should be blamed for this. 你自己應該為這件事受譴責。

▶ The procession was headed by the king **himself**. 國王親自帶領隊伍。

▶ He **himself** told me how to repair it. 他自己告訴我如何修理它。

▶ The headmaster **himself** congratulated me. 校長他親自向我道賀。

▶ *Hamlet* was written by none other than Shakespeare **himself**.

《哈姆雷特》是由莎士比亞自己——而非其他人——所寫的。

▶ He ate all the sandwiches **himself**. 他自己吃掉了所有的三明治。

▶ She **herself** baked the cake. 她自己烘烤這蛋糕。

▶ The valley **itself** is full of people. 這個山谷本身擠滿人。

▶ The painting **itself** is beautiful, but the frame is rather old-fashioned.

這幅畫本身很美，但它的畫框相當過時。

▶ We **ourselves** carried the bags. 我們自己提袋子。

▶ They found the box of treasure **themselves**. 他們自己找到了這盒寶藏。

▶ They showed the visitor around the town **themselves**. 他們自己帶著訪客參觀小鎮。

 如果刪掉用來加強語氣的反身代名詞，句子的意思仍然完整。但如果是用來表示反身用法時，則不可以省略。

▶ The Mayor (**himself**) gave us the present. 市長本人給了我們這個禮物。(強調用法，可省略)

▶ He hurt **himself** while opening the can. 開罐頭時，他傷了自己。(反身用法，不可省略)

(d) 有時，反身代名詞也可放在 be 動詞後，做主詞補語。

▶ I was upset; I wasn't quite **myself** when I shouted at her.

我心慌意亂；當我對她吼時，我很不像平常的自己。

▶ After you've taken this pill, you'll be **yourself** again. 服用這個藥丸後，你會恢復正常。

► He wasn't quite **himself** yesterday. 他昨天不太對勁。

► She wasn't **herself** when she said that. 她説那樣的話時，不像平常的她。

(e) 有時可以用反身代名詞代替人稱代名詞。

USAGE PRACTICE

► Who else was there besides **yourself**? 除了你自己之外，還有誰在那裡？（代替 you）

► This is quite a serious matter for such an efficient worker as **himself**.

對一個像他自己那樣有效率的員工而言，這是相當嚴重的事情。（代替 he）

請在每個空格中填入適當的反身代名詞。

1. Bob disguised _____ so well that even I could not recognize him.

2. I'd rather do this _____ than ask someone else to do it.

3. They enjoyed _____ very much at the seaside.

4. He applied _____ for the task of reorganizing the staff.

5. We were arguing among _____ when the chairman _____ walked into the room.

6. The players studied under the great professional coach _____ .

7. They agreed among _____ to let another person make the decision for them.

8. She felt ashamed of _____ for having lost her temper with him.

9. My parents and _____ wish all of you to make _____ at home.

10. The town _____ is very big but the people _____ live mostly on the outskirts of it.

11. The worker who was operating the machine hurt _____ very badly when his hand slipped. They saw the accident _____ and reported it to the manager. The manager _____ took the worker to the hospital.

12. "Boys, carry on with the experiment _____ ," the teacher said.

13. "Jack, do the work by _____ . You mustn't disturb Jill. She _____ has her own work to do," said his mother.

14. The dog keeps scratching _____ . Peter plans to give it a bath by _____ .

15. "We can take care of _____ . You don't need to worry," the girls _____ told their mother.

16. Does your sister know how to sew dresses _____ ? My sister _____ can sew quite well but she just doesn't have the time these days.

17. She is a deaf and dumb girl. She expresses _____ by making signs with her hands. Only her parents _____ know what she is trying to say.

18. "Pull _____ together, Mary. Your brother will be all right, and in no time he'll be _____ again," Kathy comforted her.

19. Everybody at the festival enjoyed _____ , didn't they? William and I enjoyed _____ very much.

☞ 更多相關習題請見本章應用練習 Part 12～Part 15。

Chapter 3　應用練習

PART 1

請選擇正確的代名詞填入空格中。

1. _____ (*He, Him*) was tempted to let _____ (*she, her*) do as _____ (*she, her*) liked.

2. _____ (*She, Her*) pointed an accusing finger at _____ (*he, him*) and said, "Don't let _____ (*I, me*) catch _____ (*you, it*) doing that again!"

3. Do _____ (*they, them*) know _____ (*she, her*)?

4. "It's _____ (*he, him*)! _____ (*He, Him*) scored a goal again!" the boy shouted.

5. The news reached _____ (*they, them*) just as _____ (*they, them*) were about to leave the house.

6. Look at Peter! _____ (*He, Him*) doesn't recognize _____ (*we, us*).

7. Just between the two of _____ (*we, us*), who do you think is more likely to win?

8. Her mother was worried about _____ (*she, her*), for _____ (*she, her*) had never been so late before.

9. Mr. Ford stared at _____ (*I, me*) as though _____ (*he, him*) couldn't believe his eyes.

10. Each of _____ (*we, us*) received a present from _____ (*he, him*).

11. Father wants you, Stella, and _____ (*me, I*) in his room. _____ (*He, Him*) has something to say to _____ (*we, us*).

12. Everybody can have a try, can't _____ (*we, they*)?

13. Danny, Nick, Tony, and _____ (*I, me*) are going fishing tomorrow.

14. If you are afraid of _____ (*he, him*), you can walk between William and _____ (*I, me*).

15. Snow had fallen during the night. _____ (*It, They*) covered the ground and the rooftops.

16. I wish it were _____ (*they, them*), not _____ (*we, us*) who had to go.

17. Not everyone is going, are _____ (*we, they*)?

18. Tell _____ (*she, her*) that _____ (*I, me*) have a meeting and will be late. Don't let _____ (*she, her*) know _____ (*I, me*) am working overtime.

19. You won't see much difference between _____ (*he, him*) and his brother because _____ (*they, them*) are twins.

20. Surely that isn't _____ (*she, her*) standing next to _____ (*he, him*) in the photo! I thought _____ (*they, them*) weren't on friendly terms with each other.

PART 2

請選擇正確的代名詞填入空格中。

1. He told _____ (*we, us*) stories about the wildlife of Africa. _____ (*They, It*) were very interesting.

2. He has invited _____ (*she, her*) to lunch. If I were _____ (*she, her*), I wouldn't go anywhere with _____ (*he, him*).

3. This match is between _____ (*they, them*) and _____ (*we, us*). Are _____ (*they, them*) stronger than _____ (*we, us*)?

4. It isn't _____ (*we, us*) who are to blame. It is _____ (*they, them*), but _____ (*they, them*) will surely put the blame on _____ (*we, us*).

5. Everyone has passed well except _____ (*she, her*). What do you think will happen to _____ (*she, her*)? Will _____ (*she, her*) results enable _____ (*she, her*) to be promoted?

6. She is happier than _____ (*she, her*) has been for several days. He helped to cheer _____ (*she, her*) up.

7. It was _____ (*he, him*) whom _____ (*she, her*) wanted to see, not _____ (*I, me*).

8. It was Shirley, Lily, and _____ (*I, me*) who helped _____ (*she, her*) with her work. Otherwise, _____ (*she, her*) would not have finished _____ (*it, them*).

9. He helped you more than _____ (*she, her*) helped you. Why don't you help _____ (*he, him*) too? Is _____ (*she, her*) a better friend to you than _____ (*he, him*)?

10. Nobody stayed to help _____ (*I, me*), did _____ (*he, they*)? _____ (*He, They*) couldn't care less whether _____ (*I, me*) finished my work in time.

11. A stranger gave my sisters and _____ (*I, me*) some magazines to read on our train journey to Beech Row. It was kind of _____ (*he, him*) to lend _____ (*it, them*) to _____ (*we, us*), so my elder sister thanked _____ (*he, him*).

12. It was _____ (*he, him*) who interrupted while _____ (*I, me*) was talking to _____ (*she, her*).

13. A beautiful baby! Don't you wish you could carry _____ (*him, her, it*)? Look, _____ (*he, she, it*) is gurgling happily.

14. A doctor plays a vital role in our lives. _____ (*He, It*) sees to our health and does everything _____ (*he, it*) can to cure sick people.

15. This is my new car. _____ (*He, She, It*) is lovely, isn't _____ (*he, she, it*)? Would you like to ride in _____ (*he, her, it*)? James says _____ (*he, she, it*) is a real beauty!

16. The teacher let _____ (*we, us*) go after _____ (*we, us*) had told _____ (*she, her*) the reason.

17. Were you and _____ (*he, him*) invited to the party? Everybody but Mark enjoyed the evening, didn't _____ (*he, they*)? Mark had a headache, didn't _____ (*he, him*)?

18. It wasn't _____ (*I, me*) who was to blame for breaking that vase. _____ (*I, Me*) was not near _____ (*he, it*) when _____ (*he, it*) broke. You can ask the girls; _____ (*they, them*) will tell you that _____ (*I, me*) was with _____ (*they, them*), so it couldn't have been _____ (*I, me*).

PART 3

請選擇正確的代名詞填入空格中。

1. Why did you let _____ (*he, him*) play in the match? _____ (*He, Him*) was not fit enough for it.

2. "Who's knocking at the door?" "It's only _____ (*I, me*)!"

3. Everybody is ready now, aren't _____ (*he, they*)?

4. Have you seen our magazines? _____ (*I, We*) seem to have lost _____ (*it, them*).

5. Between you and _____ (*I, me*), who do you think is better at Mathematics?

6. I think it's _____ (*I, me*) that he wants to see, not _____ (*she, her*).

7. If I were _____ (*he, him*), I wouldn't do that for all the money in the world!

8. Except for _____ (*he, him*), the rest of the children are very obedient, aren't _____ (*they, he*)?

9. _____ (*We, Us*) are going to see the film *Lord Jim* tonight. _____ (*He, It*) is a very interesting film. It was my brother who told _____ (*we, us*) about _____ (*it, them*).

10. _____ (*They, Them*) scored more goals than _____ (*we, us*) in our previous match. _____ (*We, Us*) must practice harder this time so that _____ (*we,* us) will do better than _____ (*they, them*).

11. Lily has lost the brooch that _____ (*she, her*) likes best. Please help _____ (*me, I*) find _____ (*it, they*) for _____ (*she, her*).

12. If Mother were here, _____ (*she, her*) would not let _____ (*we, us*) go to school hungry.

13. Were _____ (*they, them*) discussing that football player? Everyone says that _____ (*he, him*) is the best in the team. Almost everyone likes _____ (*he, him*), don't _____ (*he, they*)?

14. She weighs as much as _____ (*he, him*) although _____ (*she, her*) is not as tall as _____ (*he, him*).

15. Let _____ (*he, him*) have his own way. If _____ (*he, him*) does not want our advice, who will give _____ (*it, them*) to _____ (*he, him*)?

PART 4

請將粗體部分用代名詞加以取代，改寫整個句子。

1. **My uncle** told **my brother and I** about **the news**.

   → _____

2. **His parents** sent the driver to fetch **Janet** from school.

   → _____

3. **The men** spent **all their money** at the racetrack.

   → _____

4. **Karen and I** put **the clothes** into **the washing machine**.

$\rightarrow$ _____

5. **My brother** caught **a frog** in the garden yesterday.

$\rightarrow$ _____

6. **John's mother** does not allow **John** to stay up late.

$\rightarrow$ _____

7. **All the passengers** have got off **the train**.

$\rightarrow$ _____

8. **Susan** showed **the photograph** to **her friends**.

$\rightarrow$ _____

9. **The car** skidded when **Mr. Brown** was driving on the highway.

$\rightarrow$ _____

10. **Mandy and I** saw **the man** in town, but **the man** did not recognize **Mandy and I**.

$\rightarrow$ _____

11. Was **Lisa** late for **the meeting** yesterday?

$\rightarrow$ _____

12. Please tell **Peter** not to seek shelter under **the trees** during a storm.

$\rightarrow$ _____

13. The water **Lucy** drank from **the fountain** has made **Lucy** very ill.

$\rightarrow$ _____

14. **You and Rita** can wear **these sweaters** if **you and Rita** like.

$\rightarrow$ _____

15. **Robin and I** have written **all the addresses** in **this diary**.

$\rightarrow$ _____

16. **The room** is dirty. **Your brother and you** cannot sleep in **the room** until **the maid** has cleaned **the room**.

$\rightarrow$ _____

PART 5

請將粗體部分用代名詞加以取代，改寫整個句子。

1. **My sister and I** decided to visit **my aunt** this weekend.

$\rightarrow$ _____

2. **My father** told **my brother** not to make **this mistake** again.

   → _____

3. Don't tell **Lily and Sally** that **Paul and I** have forgotten to bring **the list**.

   → _____

4. **Thomas and his friends** are not going to buy **the fish tank. Thomas and his friends** say that **the fish tank** is too expensive.

   → _____

5. **The old man** bought **the shirts** from **the salesgirl**.

   → _____

6. **Miss Johnson** said that **Edward and I** should never do **such a thing** again.

   → _____

7. Have **Mark and Edwin** gone home yet? **Mark and Edwin** were just telling **my sister** that **Mark and Edwin** were tired.

   → _____

8. **Peter and Mary** had bought **the fishing line** as a birthday present for **John**.

   → _____

9. **The salesman, Mr. Lester,** was walking down the road when **Mr. Lester** bumped into **the lamp post**.

   → _____

10. **The cat** was trying to catch **the rats** when **the cat** knocked the bottle of milk over.

    → _____

11. Many of **the people** think that **many of the people** have lost their chance for **a good life**.

    → _____

12. **My brother and I** told **Shirley and her friends** that **Shirley and her friends** must find another place to do **their work**.

    → _____

13. **Mary, Peter, and Paul** say that **their mother** is not coming to the meeting because **their mother** is not feeling well.

    → _____

14. **You and your friends** are going to get into trouble if **you and your friends** persist in calling **those boys** freaks.

→ _____

15. **My friends and I** did not enjoy **the film** at all. Did **you and Janet** like **the film**?

→ _____

PART 6

請將粗體部分用代名詞加以取代，改寫整個句子。

1. **My friend's sister and my brother** have gone to see **the film**.

→ _____

2. **The woman** parked **her car** near the telephone booth and went to look for **her friends**.

→ _____

3. **The coach** told the players about **their weak points**.

→ _____

4. **Lucy** lost the key to **her house,** so **Lucy and her sister** had to wait till **their brother** returned home.

→ _____

5. **This book** is used by **those students.** I wonder if **those students** find it useful.

→ _____

6. **The message** reached **Alison and me** when **Alison and I** were playing basketball.

→ _____

7. **The children** called out to **the man** when they recognized **the man** as their uncle.

→ _____

8. **The two women** wanted to buy the same dress. **The dress** was the only one left in the shop. **The salesgirl** tried to find something else for one of the women.

→ _____

9. **Peter and I** saw the ships when **the ships** sailed into the harbor.

→ _____

10. **Mary and Jane** asked **Henry's sister** about **the new history teacher, Mr. Owings**.

→ _____

11. My brother asked **the salesman** for **the money**, so **the salesman** gave **the refund** to him.

→ _____

12. **The smugglers** hid **their contraband goods** in **a cave. The smugglers** did not know that **the**

cave would be flooded during high tide.

→ _____

13. **The results of the competition** will be published in the local newspaper. **Edward and I** are waiting anxiously for them.

→ _____

14. **The tragic news** reached **the two brothers** when **the two brothers** were in the midst of their examination.

→ _____

15. **The cakes** looked so delicious that **Molly** could not resist buying some of **the cakes**.

→ _____

16. **Barry** found **an old coin** while he was digging in the garden yesterday.

→ _____

17. **My father** is going to drive **Nancy and me** to the airport tomorrow. **Nancy and I** don't need to depend on Mr. Smith for transport.

→ _____

18. **Those obstacles** did not prevent my uncle from exploring farther up the river as **my uncle** had a very competent guide with him.

→ _____

19. **Felix and Jimmy** have told **Miss Baker** the truth, but **Miss Baker** does not believe **Felix and Jimmy** at all.

→ _____

20. **The waitress** came over to our table as soon as **my mother and I** had sat down. **The waitress** handed a menu to **my mother and me** and waited to take down our order.

→ _____

PART 7

請將粗體部分用代名詞加以取代，改寫整個句子。

1. **Nick** imitated **the call of an owl**.

→ _____

2. **My uncle** sent **Gary** to look for **Peter and I**.

→ _____

3. Do **elephants** eat nuts?

→ _____   _____

4. **My friend and I** are going to the trade fair this afternoon.

→ _____

5. **The lady** bought **several paintings** from **the artist**.

→ _____

6. **My father** dug **the flower beds** up with **a spade**.

→ _____

7. Would **Jimmy and you** tell **my aunt** about **the children**?

→ _____

8. **The cold wind** is making **their friends** shiver.

→ _____

9. **His teacher, Mr. Bright,** would not accept any of **his excuses**.

→ _____

10. **John** repaired **the rice cooker** for **his mother**.

→ _____

11. **His father and Mr. Taylor** were good friends in their school days.

→ _____

12. Don't tell **Sally and I** that **you and Fred** lost your way.

→ _____

13. **My mother and I** can't find **the hammer** anywhere. Have **you and Andrew** hidden **the hammer**?

→ _____

14. **The moths** are flying around the lights again. Please ask **Victor** to do something about **the moths**.

→ _____

15. **Mary and Catherine** brought **a piece of cake** for **Mrs. Smith**.

→ _____

16. **My brother** lost the key to **his bicycle**.

→ _____

17. **The plants** were dying, so I told **the gardener** to put **the plants** in the shade.

→ _____

18. Was **Raymond** waiting for **his taxi** yesterday?

→ _____

PART 8

請將粗體部分用所有格代名詞加以取代，改寫整個句子。

1. **Colin's shoes** look newer than **my shoes** though we bought **our shoes** at the same time. I wonder how he has kept **his shoes** in such good condition.

→ _____

2. I know this is either **your watch** or **your brother's**. It's too big to be **your sister's**.

→ _____

3. I am sharpening **my pencil**. Do you want me to sharpen **your pencils**? You may as well bring **your brother's**, too. I can sharpen **your pencils** together.

→ _____

4. **Their essays** have got mixed up with **our essays.** They should not have put **their essays** here. This shelf is **our shelf; their shelf** is just beside **our shelf**.

→ _____

5. **My typewriter** is broken. I can't use **Tracy's** because it is broken, too. May I borrow **your typewriter**?

→ _____

6. We have finished **our assignment**. They haven't even started on **their assignment**. I don't think that they will finish **their assignment** in time. What about **your assignment**?

→ _____

7. They must be friends of **your brother**'s. The car they're driving is **your brother's**.

→ _____

8. I can't find **my book** anywhere. This one is **Peter's** and that is **Julie's. Your book** is here, too. Where can **my book** be?

→ _____

9. That dog is not **our dog;** it is **their dog.** It has eaten our dog's dinner.

→ _____

10. Those friends of **David's** think that **their car** is the only car on the road. They drove **their car**

in the center of the road and did not allow **our car** to pass.

→ _____

11. He has taken **his bicycle,** not **your bicycle**. Let's go riding together. You take **your bicycle** and I'll take **my bicycle**.

→ _____

12. Our teacher has corrected **our exercises,** but not **their exercises**. She said that they did **their exercises** in such a slipshod manner that she refused to correct them.

→ _____

13. Can I borrow a racket of **your sister's**? Which of these are **your sister's**? I broke **my racket** when I was playing with Allen. He did not break **his racket**.

→ _____

14. That car is **my uncle's car**. Sometimes he gives me permission to use **his car**, unlike my sister who always refuses to let me drive **her car**.

→ _____

15. Have you seen **my bag**? I've searched everywhere but I can see only **your bag** and **Carol's**. I wonder if a friend of **your sister's** has taken **my bag** by mistake.

→ _____

16. She forgot to bring **her pen** and asked me to lend her **my pen**. But as **my pen** was broken, she borrowed **my brother's**.

→ _____

17. We have bought **our tickets** for tonight's performance but we did not buy **Richard's** and **Lily's**. They can buy **their tickets** tonight.

→ _____

18. **Their dog** is fierce but **our dog** is fiercer. **Our dog** not only barks at strangers but bites them, too. As for **their dog,** its bark is worse than its bite. **Your dog** is fiercer than **their dog**, too.

→ _____

19. This bag is **my bag**, and that is **your bag**. I know that **her bag** has a buckle which distinguishes it from **their bags** and **our bags**.

→ _____

PART 9

請將粗體部分用所有格代名詞加以取代，改寫整個句子。

1. Did you see **my spectacles** anywhere?

   → _____

2. They seem to have lost **their money**, too.

   → _____

3. **Mary's dress** has white lace on it. What is **your dress** like?

   → _____

4. No, I don't think that is **my book**. It must be **Susan's book**.

   → _____

5. Do you think you will need **our help** as well as **their help**?

   → _____

6. I think that this is **Peter's handiwork**, not **your handiwork**.

   → _____

7. He borrowed **my pencil** because he had lost **his pencil**.

   → _____

8. All **my brother's toys** have been given away to the village children.

   → _____

9. He is wearing **his new shirt**. Why aren't you wearing **your new shirt**?

   → _____

10. "Are these **your paintings**?" "No, they are not **my paintings**. They must be **my friends'**!"

    → _____

11. We must divide this equally. This will be **your share**, and that will be **our share**.

    → _____

12. I was just finishing **my homework** when she started to do **her homework**.

    → _____

13. **Lisa's glasses** look the same as **my glasses**, but **my glasses** are more expensive than **her glasses**.

    → _____

14. I hope that they have not taken **our plates** together with **their plates**. My mother told me to bring **our plates** back today.

    → _____

15. Most of the girls have brought **their food** with them. Did you bring **your lunch**, too? I brought **my lunch**, but Andy didn't bring **his lunch**. He asked me to share **my food** with him.

→ _____

PART 10

請將粗體部分用所有格代名詞加以取代，改寫整個句子。

1. He has forgotten to bring **his book**, so I am sharing **my book** with him.

→ _____

2. **My house** is nearby, but **her house** is further away.

→ _____

3. Your writing is not as neat as **her writing**, but I still prefer **your writing**.

→ _____

4. "Which of these sweets are **their sweets** and which are **our sweets**?" he asked.

→ _____

5. After Mr. Smith has marked **her test paper**, he will mark **our test papers**.

→ _____

6. "Let me have a look at **your drawing** and I'll show you **my drawing**," I told him.

→ _____

7. That house with the red roof is **Lisa's house** and **my house** is just next door.

→ _____

8. I couldn't find **my shoes**, but I saw **his shoes** under the bed, and **your shoes** were just behind the cupboard.

→ _____

9. She says that the bracelet is **her bracelet**, but I am quite sure it is **my bracelet**.

→ _____

10. I think this bag is **his bag**, not **his sister's bag**, because I have often seen him using it.

→ _____

11. As soon as we have done **our work**, we will help you finish **your work**.

→ _____

12. They gave me one of **their photos**, but I couldn't give them **my photo** as I didn't have one with me then.

$\rightarrow$ _____

13. When Lucy finished **her chocolates**, she took some of **her brother's chocolates**.

$\rightarrow$ _____

14. Eddie's shirt is being dried at the moment, so he has to wear one of **my shirts**.

$\rightarrow$ _____

15. He said he could lend us one of **his racquets**, but we brought **our rackets** just the same.

$\rightarrow$ _____

16. **Your shirt** and **his shirt** look the same except for the difference in color.

$\rightarrow$ _____

17. I checked **her answers** while she checked **my answers**.

$\rightarrow$ _____

18. We had looked into all the drawers—**her drawer**, **my drawer**, and even **his drawer**, but it wasn't in any of them.

$\rightarrow$ _____

PART 11

請將粗體部分用所有格代名詞加以取代，改寫整個句子。

1. This is **my blanket**, and that is **your blanket**.

$\rightarrow$ _____

2. He had finished eating **his apple** before I had started on **my apple**.

$\rightarrow$ _____

3. They were unwrapping **their presents** while we were unwrapping **our presents**.

$\rightarrow$ _____

4. She is wearing **her spectacles**. Where are **your spectacles**?

$\rightarrow$ _____

5. That knife is **Martin's**, but those bags are **Maria's**.

$\rightarrow$ _____

6. **All his friends' paintings** have names on them.

$\rightarrow$ _____

7. Are these **your handkerchiefs** or **my handkerchiefs**?

$\rightarrow$ _____

8. I think this is **Ben's and William's work** and that is **Peter's work**.

→ _____

9. We have been to **John's house**, but we haven't been to **Emma's house**.

→ _____

10. Do you need **our table** as well as **her table**?

→ _____

11. That cat is **the girl's**. It is not **their cat**.

→ _____

12. Are these **our cups**? We do not want to use **their cups**.

→ _____

13. **Mary's sweater** looks newer than **my sweater** though both of us bought **our sweaters** at the same time.

→ _____

PART 12

請在空格中填入合適的反身代名詞。

1. The contractors agreed among _____ not to find any other worker. They wanted to let that man do the work _____ .

2. Simon organized the party _____ . It was small, but we enjoyed _____ very much.

3. "Suit _____ , sir. There are many people who will be beside _____ with happiness to possess this. You can take it or leave it," he said.

4. I am not tired _____ , but I think that my little brother is. He walked all the way home by _____ and refused to be carried. You _____ would admire his determination, too.

5. Everybody enjoyed _____ , didn't they? Even Richard, who is very conservative, enjoyed _____ , too.

6. As my brother _____ cannot accompany me, I will go by _____ . My sister went by _____ before and she wasn't afraid.

7. He has been there _____ . He says that the place _____ is beautiful but the hotels are dirty. Perhaps he _____ is too fussy.

8. The boys _____ were eager to cook, but none of them knew how to clean a chicken by _____ .

9. She reminded her students to behave _____ during the inspector's visit. Otherwise, she _____ would get the blame for their misconduct.

10. People should guard _____ from danger, but there are times when danger _____ appeals to them.

11. Do the work _____, you lazy boy. Do you want me to get your father _____ here to make you do so? You cannot always ask others to do it for you because they have their own work to do _____.

12. Recently he composed a song _____. The lyrics _____ were beautiful but the music was not very good.

13. Jim and I agreed between _____ to paint the fence. Jim _____ will start from that end and I _____ will start from here.

14. I baked this cake by _____. Wouldn't you like to taste it _____? Have you ever baked cakes by _____?

15. She was very pleased with _____ when she received the prize from the Chief Minister _____. Her parents were also beside _____ with joy when they heard of her success.

16. He cannot express _____ clearly in English. He is trying hard to learn the language by _____ and his sister is helping him though she _____ is not very good at it.

17. He checked the accounts _____, so they must be correct. If there had been any mistakes, he would have corrected them.

PART 13

請在空格中填入合適的反身代名詞。

1. We _____ did not know what was happening there.

2. The boys shouted and cheered _____ at the football match.

3. You _____ knew about this, but none of you bothered to tell me.

4. I found out about this incident from Tom _____.

5. My sister, Stella, and my cousin baked these jam tarts all by _____.

6. I did not do it by _____. It was Jimmy _____ who helped me with it.

7. Jenny and I made all the arrangements by _____. The others did not bother to stir _____ to help.

8. I _____ suggested the idea of going on a picnic. In the end, they went off by _____

without telling me.

9. We were all by _____ in the house when Mr. Wilson _____ dropped in for a visit.

10. I tried to convince _____ that I hadn't been quite _____ when I lost my temper.

11. "How many were there on the bus besides _____, Jane?" "There were twelve others besides _____."

12. The dog nearly killed _____ when it dashed across the road. Paul was almost beside _____ with fright.

13. Don't lose _____ in the woods. Even the most experienced hikers _____ can lose their way.

14. We argued among _____ over this matter. Finally, I suggested that we should approach the manager _____.

PART 14

請在空格中填入合適的反身代名詞。

1. The old man locked _____ in the room and took out his money box.

2. He was counting the money aloud to _____ when there was a knock at the door.

3. We prepared _____ for the worst to happen; there was no way out for us.

4. The manager told me this _____, but I couldn't believe him.

5. The magician turned _____ into a bird and flew off.

6. "Look after _____, Nelson," his mother told him.

7. Brenda bought _____ a dress and a scarf.

8. He _____ told me he wouldn't be going to the party.

9. When I told her my problem, she _____ offered to help me out.

10. We enjoyed _____ very much at the barbecue given by Mrs. Ritchie _____.

11. "Don't blame _____ for this, boys," he comforted them.

12. The boys argued among _____ as to who should be the leader of the group.

13. I saw Peter sitting by _____ near the river an hour ago.

14. The cat licked _____ clean after eating the fish.

15. The scenery _____ is beautiful, but the climb up there is exhausting.

16. They shared the money among _____, each getting about $55.

17. I felt very proud of _____ as the King _____ put the medal around my neck.

18. Nobody can be sure of _____ when it is a matter of life and death _____ .

19. The group composed the song _____ . The music _____ is good, but the lyrics are rather meaningless.

20. "Help _____ , girls. I made the cakes and biscuits _____ , and there are plenty more of them," she said.

PART 15

請在空格中填入合適的反身代名詞。

1. The baby scratched _____ with his fingernails.

2. He bought _____ a new shirt yesterday. He looked so different with it on that even his mother _____ nearly failed to recognize him.

3. They are feeling very pleased with _____ . Aren't you feeling pleased with _____ , too?

4. I _____ will take you all on a tour of the city. I'm sure that you will enjoy _____ .

5. The Minister of Education _____ paid a visit to our school yesterday.

6. You ought to be ashamed of _____ , girls. Even Helen _____ wouldn't do such a thing.

7. We reminded _____ that Wednesday was the important day.

8. The cat nearly killed _____ by climbing into the water pipe.

9. He doesn't trust _____ with the money.

10. All of us painted the fence _____ .

11. The bus drivers argued among _____ whether they should go on strike.

12. Did Mrs. Jones _____ tell you the news? I wish I could have told you earlier _____ .

13. The members of the club contributed the money _____ .

14. Tom and Robin built the boat all by _____ . Mr. Strong _____ had seen them building it.

15. We felt so sorry for _____ that even Father _____ could not console us.

PART 16

請根據提示，在空格中填入合適的所有格代名詞或反身代名詞。

1. She scratched _____ (she) on a rusty nail just now.

2. He gave _____ (*his racket*) to his brother and borrowed _____ (*my racket*) for _____ (*he*).

3. The cat is cleaning _____ (*it*).

4. We are helping _____ (*we*) to the food. Have you had _____ (*your food*) yet?

5. He reminded _____ (*he*) about _____ (*his homework*). He will do it all by _____ (*he*) this time.

6. I stopped _____ (*me*) from taking _____ (*her flowers*).

7. She has taken _____ (*that lady's umbrella*) by mistake.

8. The baby has cried _____ (it) to sleep.

9. _____ (*The students' concert*) was very entertaining. I went to it _____ (*I*) yesterday.

10. I have borrowed _____ (*Mary's bicycle*), and he has borrowed _____ (*Allen's bicycle*). We don't think that we will lose _____ (*we*) on the way to Alice's house.

11. The deaf-and-dumb girl has taught _____ (*she*) how to lip-read. I think she can understand our message, but we cannot understand _____ (*her message*).

12. All you boys should be ashamed of _____ (*you*). The principal _____ (*he*) is very angry at what you have done.

13. They argued among _____ (*they*) whether to bring _____ (*their magazines*) to class or not.

14. Aunt Jane _____ (*she*) does not know what to do about _____ (*her work*). We are going to help her _____ (*we*).

Chapter 4 關係代名詞

4-0 基本概念

關係代名詞引導形容詞子句修飾先行詞。關係代名詞 who、whom 和 whose 用在先行詞是「人」的時候，關係代名詞 which 則用在先行詞是「動物或事物」的時候，而 that 則在先行詞是「人、動物或事物」時都可以使用。關係代名詞也可以視為是用來連結兩個指涉同一個人或事物的句子。

4-1 關係代名詞 who、whom、whose

(a) 關係代名詞 who 引導形容詞子句，修飾的先行詞是人，且通常作形容詞子句的主詞，後接動詞。

USAGE PRACTICE

▶ The man **who** has just come in is a police officer. 剛剛走進來的男子是個警官。

▶ Could you recognize the man **who** spoke to you last night?
　你認得出昨晚與你談話的男子嗎？

▶ That boy **who** spoke to you just now is a friend of mine.
　剛才和你講話的那個男孩是我的一個朋友。

▶ The child **who** paints the best picture will be given a prize.
　畫出最好的圖畫的小朋友會得獎。

▶ The girl **who** won the prize is my friend. 得獎的那個女孩是我的朋友。

▶ That is the person **who** ran away with her handbag. 那就是搶她手提包而逃跑的人。

▶ Is that the woman **who** complained to you? 那是向你抱怨的女人嗎？

▶ The lady **who** lives here is away at the moment. 住在這裡的女士目前不在。

▶ The boy **who** stole the bicycle has been caught. 偷腳踏車的那個男孩已經被抓了。

(b) whom 是 who 的受格，它常用在名詞或代名詞之前，可以作形容詞子句中動詞的受詞。

USAGE PRACTICE

▶ The lawyer **whom** he consulted is quite well-known. 他徵詢意見的律師相當有名。

▶ The man **whom** the police caught was sentenced to two years in jail.

警方抓到的那個男子被判坐牢兩年。

▶ The woman **whom** we saw just now is Lucy's mother.　我們剛剛看到的女人是露西的媽媽。

▶ The baby **whom** the gangsters kidnapped was not the real prince.

歹徒們綁架的嬰兒並非真正的王子。

(c) whom 也可以作形容詞子句中介系詞的受詞，介系詞通常置於關係代名詞之前，
但也常見放在子句的句尾。

USAGE PRACTICE

▶ That is the girl **to whom** I handed the money.　那就是那個女孩，我把錢交給了她。

▶ Where is the lady **to whom** you introduced me just now?

你剛剛介紹我給她認識的女士在哪裡？

▶ We are the people **to whom** you must come when you are in trouble.

我們是當你有困難時一定要來找的人。

▶ The girl **whom** he was talking **to** just now is my friend.

剛剛在和他談話的女孩是我的朋友。

▶ He said that the woman **whom** we were looking **for** had gone home.

他說我們正在尋找的那個女人已經回家去了。

▶ He is the man **on whom** the managing director relies.　他就是總經理倚重的人。

▶ I know the man **whom** they are hiding **from**.　我認識他們正在躲避不想見到的人。

▶ Those are the boys **with whom** you will have to live.

那些是你將必須和他們共同生活的男孩們。

▶ That is the family **with whom** I am staying.　那是我寄住的家庭。

▶ That is the boy **whom** Tom left the bag **with**.　那就是那個男孩，湯姆把袋子留給了他。

▶ She is the person **of whom** I have heard so much.　她是那個我經常聽到別人提及的人。

▶ She doesn't know the person **whom** we are talking **about**.

她不認識我們正在談論的那個人。

▶ We met the writer **whom** everyone was talking **about**.

我們遇見大家都在討論的那個作家。

在非正式的用法中，whom 在當關係代名詞時，只要不是直接用在介系詞之後，幾乎都會被 who 來取代。

▶ She's just the girl **who** I want to be **with**. 她就是我希望能在一起的女孩。

▶ I don't think he is the man **on whom** you can depend. 我覺得他不是一個可以倚靠的男人。
（不可用 who 取代，除非將 on 移至句尾）

(d) whose 是 who 的所有格，後面必須接名詞，以表示「擁有、關係或個人特質」。

USAGE PRACTICE

▶ The man **whose** car was stolen has reported the case to the police.

這個車子被偷的男子已經向警方報案了。（表示擁有）

▶ The little girl **whose** dress was dirty dared not go home.

這個衣服髒了的小女孩不敢回家。（表示擁有）

▶ Is that the person **whose** house was robbed last night?

那是昨晚家裡遭人搶劫的那個人嗎？（表示擁有）

▶ That is the artist **whose** paintings are on exhibition.

那就是畫作正在展出的藝術家。（表示擁有）

▶ Do you know the shopkeeper **whose** shop was broken into?

你認識商店被闖入的那位店主嗎？（表示擁有）

▶ He consoled the lady **whose** husband had been killed in the accident.

他安慰那位丈夫死於意外的女士。（表示關係）

▶ The boy **whose** sister is a nurse has decided to become a doctor.

這個男孩的姊姊是護士，他已決定要成為一位醫生。（表示關係）

▶ Show me a person **whose** wisdom is greater than Solomon's.

介紹一個智慧高於索羅門的人給我。（表示個人特質）

▶ He is a man **whose** patience is very limited. 他是個耐心非常有限的人。（表示個人特質）

---

 whose 引導的形容詞子句也可以修飾表示動物或事物的先行詞，詳見 **4-2**。

▶ I saw a cat **whose** eyes were of two different colors. 我看見一隻貓，牠兩隻眼睛顏色不一樣。

請在空格中填入 who 或 whom 以完成句子。不要用非正式的 who 來取代正式的 whom。

基礎文法寶典 ❶
Essential English Usage & Grammar

1. The person _____ was standing next to me seemed very nervous.

2. The girl about _____ he was talking lives near my house.

3. Is he the boy _____ you gave the parcel to?

4. Women _____ nurse the wounded and the dying on battlefields are to be respected and admired.

5. Monica is the girl _____ the committee has chosen to be the chairperson of the club.

6. Can you point out the person _____ gave you the message?

7. Is there anyone here _____ can help me carry the books to the classroom?

8. Get it back from the person _____ you gave it to.

9. The doctor _____ prescribed this medicine for me also advised me to rest.

10. Where is the boy _____ you are supposed to meet?

11. The person to _____ this library is dedicated was on our school's board.

12. The candidate _____ he interviewed last week is starting work today.

☞ 更多相關習題請見本章應用練習 Part 1～Part 3。

4-2 關係代名詞 which

(a) which 修飾的先行詞是動物或事物，可以作形容詞子句的主詞，後接動詞。

USAGE PRACTICE

▶ That is the house **which** caught fire last night. 那是昨晚失火的房子。

▶ Those are the huts **which** are to be pulled down. 那些就是要拆掉的小屋。

▶ Is this the dog **which** bit the man? 這是咬了那男子的狗嗎？

▶ The machine **which** sprays insecticide on the crops is broken.
　噴灑殺蟲劑在農作物上的機器壞掉了。

(b) which 可以當形容詞子句中動詞或介系詞的受詞，後面通常接名詞或代名詞。如果是當介系詞的受詞，該介系詞可以放在 which 之前，也可以放在形容詞子句的後面。

USAGE PRACTICE

▶ The book **which** you want is on the table. 你要的書在桌上。

▶ She decided to buy the dress **which** she had seen in the shop.

她決定要買她在店裡看見的那一件洋裝。

▶ The evidence **which** the police found is sufficient to have her arrested.

警察發現的証據足以將她逮捕。

▶ The animal **which** they saw wasn't a deer. 他們看到的動物不是一隻鹿。

▶ The book **about which** they were talking has been banned.

他們當時在談論的那本書已經被禁了。

▶ This is the dog **which** the neighbors were talking **about**. 這是鄰居們過去在談論的狗。

▶ The dress **of which** she was very fond has been given away to her cousin.

她過去很喜歡的洋裝已經被送給她的堂妹。

▶ The box **in which** he kept his money is gone. 他放錢的箱子不見了。

▶ That is the bungalow **which** we usually stay **at**. 那就是我們經常暫住的小屋。

▶ The place **which** I am going **to** is very far away. 我要去的地方非常遙遠。

(c) which 有時候也可以當作表示「一個團體的人」的先行詞。

USAGE PRACTICE

▶ The team **which** played for Prince Avenue won the match.

代表王子大街的隊伍贏得了比賽。

4-3 關係代名詞 that

(a) 可以用 that 代替 who，有時 that 比 who 的意思更清楚、明確。

USAGE PRACTICE

▶ He knows the man **that** sells cakes in that shop. 他認識在那家店賣蛋糕的男人。

▶ The man **that** looks after the garden is ill. 照顧花園的那個男子病了。

▶ The girl **that** won the prize is my friend. 得獎的女孩是我的朋友。

▶ My sister **that** is in Richtown sent me a gift. 我在瑞奇鎮的姊姊寄了一個禮物給我。

▶ My friend **that** was with me saw it, too. 那時和我在一起的朋友也看見了。

▶ The scout **that** saved a child from drowning was awarded a medal.

救了溺水小孩的童子軍被頒發了一個獎章。

▶ The robber **that** had escaped from the train has been caught.

從火車上逃走的強盜已經被捕了。

(b) that 也可以代替 whom，作形容詞子句中動詞或介系詞的受詞。

USAGE PRACTICE

▶ The man **that** we saw had a scar on his forehead. 我們看到的那個男人額頭上有個疤。
▶ The boys **that** he taught last year have passed their examination.

他去年教的男孩們已經通過考試。

▶ Those are the people **that** we met yesterday. 那些就是我們昨天遇見的人們。
▶ The artist **that** you want to see is over there. 你想要見的藝術家在那裡。
▶ There is the woman **that** we heard the story **from**. 告訴我們這個故事的女人就在那裡。
▶ The boy **that** you told us **about** is here to see you.

你跟我們提過的那個男孩來這裡看你了。

▶ The boy **that** you quarreled **with** has disappeared. 和你爭論的男孩不見了。
▶ The person **that** I spoke **to** didn't know the way. 和我講話的那個人不認識路。
▶ This is the person **that** she was afraid **of**. 這就是她之前害怕的人。
▶ We met the singer **that** everyone is talking **about**. 我們遇見大家都在談論的歌手。

 但是，that 不可以取代置於介系詞後的 whom。

▶ The artist **with whom** he is talking is very talented. 和他講話的藝術家很有天份。
(×with that)
▶ The boy **against whom** you have to play is very strong. 要和你對打的男孩很強壯。
(×against that)
▶ The girl **with whom** I discussed the matter is her cousin. 和我討論事情的女孩是她的表妹。
(×with that)
▶ There's the girl **to whom** I was talking yesterday. 那是昨天和我講話的女孩。
(×to that)

(c) that 可以用來代替當作主格或受格的 which，修飾動物和無生命事物的先行詞。

USAGE PRACTICE

▶ The sheep **that** are up the hill belong to Mr. Jones. 山坡上的羊是瓊斯先生所有。

▶ The team **that** won the match was presented with the trophy by the Governor.

贏得比賽的隊伍由州長頒發獎盃。

▶ The dog **that** he bought is very fierce. 他買的那隻狗很兇猛。

▶ The puppy **that** he wanted has been given to somebody else.

他想要的小狗已被送給其他人了。

▶ The album **that** I bought some time ago has been misplaced.

我之前買的專輯不知道被錯放在何處。

▶ He snatched away the book **that** the boy was reading. 他搶走那男孩正在讀的書。

▶ This is the place **that** the man was telling us **about**.

這就是那個男子過去常跟我們提過的地方。

▶ This is the hotel **that** he stayed **in** last month. 這是他上個月投宿的旅館。

 但是，that 不可以取代置於介系詞後的 which。

> ▶ The book **from which** this page is torn is lost. 被撕下這頁的書遺失了。(×from that)
> ▶ The squirrel **at which** he was aiming disappeared from sight. 他正瞄準的松鼠消失不見了。
> (×at that)

(d) 先行詞含有 all、everything、nothing、none、much、not any... 等字時，常用 that 來引導形容詞子句。

USAGE PRACTICE

▶ There is nothing **that** I can do to help. 沒有我能幫得上忙的地方。

▶ He has everything **that** money can buy. 他擁有金錢能買得到的一切東西。

▶ There's not much **that** can be done about this. 這件事沒什麼可以插手的。

▶ This is all **that** I can do. 我所能做的就是這樣而已。

▶ All **that** worries him is his father's objection to it. 唯一令他擔心的事就是他父親反對。

(e) 先行詞前面若有最高級形容詞時，也常用 that 引導形容詞子句。

USAGE PRACTICE

▶ He is the greatest writer **that** ever lived. 他是迄今為止最偉大的作家。

▶ She is the most talented singer **that** I have ever heard. 她是我聽過最有天份的歌手。

▶ She is the kindest girl **that** I know.　她是我認識最親切的女孩。

▶ This is one of the most exciting games **that** we have ever played.

這是我們曾經參與過最刺激的比賽之一。

▶ It is one of the most exciting stories **that** have ever been written.

這是有史以來寫得最刺激的故事之一。

▶ It was the most appetizing meal **that** we've ever had.

它是我們曾經吃過最令人垂涎的一餐。

 在此用法中，必須注意使用正確的動詞形式。

▶ This is one of the best films **that** have been produced so far.
這是目前已經製作出最好的影片之一。（先行詞是複數名詞 films）

▶ This is the best film **that** has been produced so far.
這是目前已經製作出最好的影片。（先行詞是單數名詞 film）

(f) 先行詞含序數或 last、only 等字時，通常使用 that。

USAGE PRACTICE

▶ This is the only novel **that** is worth reading.　這是唯一值得一讀的小說。

▶ The last thing **that** I will do is to take revenge on him.　我絕對不會報復他。

▶ This will be the first and the last time **that** I shall be helping you.

這將會是我第一次，也是最後一次幫助你。

請在空格中填入適當的關係代名詞 who、whom、whose、which 或 that 來完成句子。請注意 that 僅限用於一定要使用的情況，同時也避免用非正式的 who 來取代正式的 whom。

1. She has donated all the cakes _____ she baked yesterday to the fair.

2. We saw the film _____ you said was the best one _____ you had ever seen.

3. The boy to _____ I lent the CD did not come to school today.

4. This is the man _____ said that he was an electrical engineer.

5. I spoke to the person _____ was in charge of the team.

6. The boy from _____ I borrowed this book wants it back soon.

7. David and Charles have a tree house in _____ they spend most of their free time.

8. The girl _____ you were telling us about yesterday is here to see you.

9. I know the girl _____ father owns the big white house on top of the hill.

10. We said "Hello" to the boy _____ lives in the opposite house.

11. Where is the girl _____ was so rude to my little sister?

12. The man _____ stole my watch and wallet has been caught by the police.

13. We gave a farewell party to the teacher _____ is leaving the school next month.

14. The man _____ car was involved in the accident was taken to the hospital.

15. I know a girl _____ hobby is collecting shells.

16. I answered the telephone _____ had been ringing for several minutes.

17. The lady _____ wrote this book has come to speak at the Women's Union meeting.

18. The house _____ had been partly destroyed during the war is being repaired now.

19. Thomas and Gary have a very large stamp collection _____ contains many beautiful, rare stamps.

20. The bird _____ you see over there on the fence is a sparrow.

☞ 更多相關習題請見本章應用練習 Part 4～Part 7。

4-4 關係代名詞的省略

(a) that、whom 和 which 在形容詞子句中作動詞或介系詞的受詞時，通常可以省略且不影響句意，形成所謂的「聯繫子句 (contact clause)」。

USAGE PRACTICE

▶ The magazines (**which**) I bought yesterday are old copies.　昨天我買的雜誌是舊書。

▶ The book (**which**) I am reading is very interesting.　我正在讀的這本書非常有趣。

▶ The book (**which**) I borrowed from the library is missing.
　我從圖書館借來的那本書不見了。

▶ Has anyone seen the book (**which**) I was reading just now?
　有人看到我剛才在讀的那本書嗎？

▶ Show me the picture (**that**) you have painted.　給我看你畫好的圖。

▶ He has just sold one of the paintings (**that**) he did during his stay in Tokyo.
　他剛剛賣掉他在東京停留期間所畫的作品其中一幅。

▶ The fifty-dollar bill (**which**) he found was a counterfeit one.　他發現的五十元鈔票是假鈔。

▶ The radio (**that**) she bought yesterday cost a hundred and fifty dollars.

她昨天買的收音機價值一百五十元。

▶ I have given him everything (**that**) he needs. 我已經給他所需要的一切。

▶ The house (**which**) they are living in is said to be haunted. 據說他們現在住的房子鬧鬼。

▶ This is the man (**that**) I spoke to just now. 這是我剛才跟他講話的男子。

▶ That is the man (**whom**) I was telling you about the other day.

那就是我前幾天跟你提到的那個男人。

▶ The clerk (**whom**) you want to see is on leave today. 你想見的職員今天休假。

▶ He came home with a puppy (**that**) he had found by the road.

他帶著他在路邊發現的小狗回家。

請利用連繫子句的概念，以省略關係代名詞的方式來將兩個句子合併為一句。

1. The mistake is very serious. He made the mistake.

   → _____

2. The handbag contains a lot of money. She lost the handbag.

   → _____

3. The person is a total stranger. I am writing to him.

   → _____

4. The girl has disappeared. I took this from her.

   → _____

5. The cake is very delicious. My sister baked it this morning.

   → _____

6. The watch is a brand-new one. She is wearing it.

   → _____

7. The lady is my mother. You helped her yesterday.

   → _____

8. The boy has brought it back. I entrusted the bag to him.

   → _____

9. The songs will be sung at the concert. He composed the songs.

→ _____

10. She has bought all the things for the party. She needs them.

→ _____

11. The bench is still wet with paint. He is sitting on it.

→ _____

12. The album is my brother's. They are looking at it.

→ _____

13. Has the knife been put in a safe place? You sharpened it just now.

→ _____

4-5 限定用法與非限定用法

(a) 限定用法有限定、修飾的作用，使先行詞更具體、明確。在此用法中，關係代名詞引導的子句不可任意省略，否則句意會不完整；而先行詞與關係代名詞之間不加逗點。

USAGE PRACTICE

▶ The man **who** committed the crime has been arrested. 犯案的男子已經被逮捕了。

▶ The man **who** sold it to me said it was washable. 把它賣給我的男子說它是可以洗的。

▶ That is the girl **who** won first prize in the elocution contest.
那是贏得朗誦比賽第一名的女孩。

▶ The woman **whom** we saw had a mole on her left arm.
我們看到的那個婦人在左手臂上有一顆痣。

▶ This is the man **whose** bravery stopped the raging bull.
是這男子的勇敢阻止了狂怒的公牛。

▶ The boy **whose** brother you fought with wants to see you.
那個男孩想見你，他的弟弟和你打過架。

▶ The girl **whose** hand was bleeding profusely fainted.
這個女孩昏倒了，她的手正在大量出血。

▶ That is the hotel **which** burned down last night. 那是昨晚燒毀的旅館。

▶ The film **which** they saw is still showing at the Pavilion.
他們之前看的影片現在仍然在展示館中放映。

> ▶ He snatched away the book **that** the boy was reading. 他奪走那男孩正在讀的書。

(b) 非限定用法是對意義已經明確的先行詞做附加說明，因此即使省略關係代名詞引導的子句，句意仍然完整。此用法中的關係代名詞不可以省略，而且不可以用 that 來取代；而先行詞與關係代名詞之間要加逗點。

USAGE PRACTICE

▶ One of the beggars, **who** was blind, has been killed in an accident.

其中一個乞丐已在一次意外中死亡，他是個盲人。

▶ Ken, **whom** we met at the fair, was wearing a red shirt.

肯穿著一件紅襯衫，我們在市集遇見過他。

▶ My father, **who** is in New York, sent me a gift. 我爸爸寄了一個禮物給我，他現在在紐約。

▶ Rita and Alice, **whom** we met on the way, told us the news.

麗塔和愛麗絲告訴我們這個消息，我們在路上遇見她們。

▶ Greg, **whom** the police released yesterday, has gone back to his hometown.

葛瑞格已回到家鄉，他昨天被警方釋放。

▶ Elisa, **whose** English is very fluent, was chosen to represent the school.

艾麗莎被選為學校的代表，她的英文非常流利。

▶ Sonia, **whose** purse was stolen, is crying.

索妮亞在哭，她的皮包被偷了。

▶ Danny, **whose** father is a pilot, wants to be a pilot, too.

丹尼也想成為一個飛行員，他的父親是個飛行員。

▶ Eddie, **whose** brother is in my class, is going to Manito City.

艾迪正要去曼尼突市，他弟弟在我的班上。

▶ Mr. Smith, **whose** garden is really beautiful, has won first prize in the Flower Show.

史密斯先生贏得花展的首獎，他的花園真漂亮。

▶ Mr. Jones, **whose** eyesight is failing, has to wear glasses.

瓊斯先生得戴眼鏡了，他的視力漸漸衰退。

▶ Mrs. Johnson, **whose** child is one of his students, wants to speak to him.

強森太太想要跟他談話，她的孩子是他的一個學生。

(c) which 引導非限定用法的關係子句，可用來修飾前面的整個子句。

USAGE PRACTICE

▶ She often sleeps the whole day, **which** is what she did yesterday.

她常常睡上一整天，她昨天就這麼做了。

▶ The escaped prisoner decided to give himself up, **which** was the best thing to do.

這逃犯決定要自首，這是最佳的選擇。

▶ He offered to drive us home, **which** was very kind of him.

他表示願意載我們回家，真是好心。

(d) that 不可以取代非限定用法中的 who、whom、which 等。

USAGE PRACTICE

▶ Mr. McCain, **who** is a senator, is also a writer. 麥肯先生是參議員，也是作家。(不可用 that)

▶ Her cousin, **whom** you know, has left. 她的表哥已經離開了，你認識他。(不可用 that)

(e) 限定用法或非限定用法的取捨，要看句子情境而定。相同的句子加上逗點形成非限定用法之後，意思會略有不同。

USAGE PRACTICE

▶ The dog, **which** belongs to Mr. Jones, is very fierce. 這隻狗很兇猛，牠是瓊斯先生的。

（ 非限定用法，表示只有一隻狗，不會混淆，所以不需限定。）

▶ The dog **that/which** belongs to Mr. Jones is very fierce. 屬於瓊斯先生的狗很兇猛。

（ 限定用法，表示有兩隻以上的狗，有混淆的可能，所以需限定說明是瓊斯先生的狗。）

▶ The express train, **which** leaves New City in the evening, is always crowded.

那班快車總是很擁擠，它在傍晚駛離新市。

（ 非限定用法，表示只有那班快車，不會混淆，所以不需限定。）

▶ The express train **that/which** leaves New City in the evening is always crowded.

在傍晚駛離新市的快車總是很擁擠。

（ 限定用法，表示有兩班以上的快車，所以需限定說明是駛離新市的車。）

 小練習

請在空格中填入適當的關係代名詞 who、whom、whose 和 which。請不要使用 that，同時也避免用非正式的 who 來取代正式的 whom。

1. Miss Jacobs, _____ brother is a doctor, is a good friend of mine.

2. The Suez Canal, through _____ so many ships pass, was closed during the war.

3. Mr. Lester, with _____ we traveled to Newtown, has just sent us an invitation card to his wedding.

4. Raymond, _____ music you liked so much, is also a very good singer.

5. The bell, _____ went off just now, is for the boys to assemble on the school field.

6. Mr. Rogers, _____ is in charge of the choir, has asked us to attend the rehearsal this afternoon.

7. Jim, with _____ we were working yesterday, did not turn up today.

8. Mr. Collins, _____ tools you just found in the shed, has come back to claim them.

9. The sky, _____ was very cloudy this morning, has cleared.

10. English, _____ is a universal language, is not very difficult to learn.

11. My little brother, _____ you see over there, is very good at chess.

12. That man over there, at _____ the dogs are barking, is an old school friend of my father.

13. Monica, _____ I had not seen since she was a child, has already graduated from high school.

14. The meeting, _____ lasted for one and a half hours, was held to elect a new committee.

15. My friend, with _____ we went to the movies, took us all home after the show.

16. I would like to speak to your sister, _____ is in the same class as my sister.

17. My little sister, _____ cat is missing, has been crying the whole morning.

18. The city of Lincoln, _____ was named after President Abraham Lincoln, is the capital of Nebraska.

19. Paul, _____ I had not seen for several weeks, has gone to his uncle's house.

20. The Brooklyn Bridge, _____ was built at least one hundred years ago, is going to be repainted.

☞ 更多相關習題請見本章應用練習 Part 8～Part 10。

4-6 非限定關係子句的其他用法

(a) 在非限定用法中，可以用「（代）名詞＋介系詞＋關係代名詞」的結構。在此結構中，介系詞通常用 of 表示「關係」或「所有」，關係代名詞則多用 whom 或

which。此結構除了用名詞或代名詞，還可以用數詞等。

USAGE PRACTICE

▶ We discovered an old map, **the corners of which** were torn.

我們發現一張舊地圖，它的角都破損了。

▶ They gave him a sword, **the handle of which** was made of ivory.

他們給了他一把劍，劍柄是用象牙做的。

▶ The pen, **the nib of which** was crooked, was thrown away. 這枝筆筆尖彎了，被丟掉了。

▶ In the garden there is an old tree, **the trunk of which** is hollow.

花園裡有一棵老樹，樹幹是中空的。

▶ We bought a huge melon, **half of which** was eaten by Tom.

我們買了一個大香瓜，其中有一半被湯姆吃掉了。

▶ He bought some apples, **half of which** were bad.

他買了一些蘋果，其中有半數是壞的。

▶ The bananas, **three quarters of which** were overripe, were thrown away.

四分之三的香蕉過熟，全都被丟掉了。

▶ There were many books on the table, **some of which** belonged to him.

桌上有許多書，其中有一些是他的。

▶ They had a green fence, **parts of which** were already bleached by the sun.

他們有一道綠色圍籬，其中部分已被太陽晒成白色了。

▶ The mother dog guarded her puppies, **two of which** were blind.

這隻母狗保護著她的小狗，其中兩隻瞎了。

▶ The boys, **three of whom** were hurt, were rescued by a helicopter.

這些男孩們被直昇機救了，他們其中有三個人受傷。

 請比較下列句子。

▶ There were four passengers in the taxi. Three of them were sitting in the back.
計程車裡有四個乘客，有三個乘客坐在後座。（兩句都是獨立子句）

▶ There were four passengers in the taxi, **three of whom** were sitting in the back.
計程車裡有四個乘客，其中三個坐在後座。（一個主要子句加上一個非限定子句）

▶ I bought a dozen eggs. Two of them were bad.
我買了一打雞蛋，有兩個壞掉了。（兩句都是獨立子句）

▶ I bought a dozen eggs, **two of which** were bad.

我買了一打雞蛋，其中兩個壞掉了。（一個主要子句加上一個非限定子句）

▶ We caught five big fish. We gave two to the old man.

我們捕獲五條大魚，我們送給了那個老人兩條。（兩句都是獨立子句）

▶ We caught five big fish, **two of which** we gave to the old man.

我們捕獲五條大魚，其中兩條我們送給了那個老人。（一個主要子句加上一個非限定子句）

(b) 此結構也可以用「介系詞＋關係代名詞＋（代）名詞」。

USAGE PRACTICE

▶ The soldiers, **of whom only half** were armed, retreated.

這些軍人撤退了，其中只有一半有武裝。

▶ About <u>ten students</u> were chosen, **of whom two** were from our class and **five** from his

class. 大約有十名學生入選，其中兩個來自我們班、五個來自他的班。

 此類的句子結構有時會很不自然，且意思容易混淆，可改用較好的方式表達同樣的涵義。

▶ About ten students were chosen. Two of them were from our class and five from his class.

大約有十名學生入選。其中兩個來自我們班、五個來自他的班。

請以正確的關係代名詞用法來合併下列句子。

1. He bought a big bunch of grapes. Half the grapes were sour.

→ _____

2. She found the box. The cover of the box was dented.

→ _____

3. I have thrown away the book. The pages of the book were torn.

→ _____

4. I examined those antiques. A few of those antiques were priceless.

→ _____

5. She has sent the shoes to the cobbler. The heels of the shoes were worn-out.

→ _____

6. A large crowd watched the play. Most of the play was hard to understand.

→ _____

7. We enjoyed eating the food. All the food was delicious.

→ _____

8. The cat gave birth to three kittens. Two of the kittens were white and brown.

→ _____

9. He sent the watch to the repair shop. The spring of the watch was broken.

→ _____

10. This is the dress. The hem of the dress had been let down.

→ _____

11. The box has been thrown away. The bottom of the box had dropped out.

→ _____

12. The book is not interesting at all. The cover of the book is very attractive.

→ _____

13. A wallet has been found. The inside of the wallet contained a photograph and some money.

→ _____

14. Mother had baked a huge birthday cake. Half of the cake was covered with cherries.

→ _____

15. She had bought a kilogram of grapes. Three quarters of the grapes were rotten.

→ _____

16. The carpenter has repaired the table. A leg of the table which was broken.

→ _____

17. The players were victorious in the match. Three of the players were veterans.

→ _____

18. These children will take part in the play. A few of these children are less than six years old.

→ _____

☞ 更多相關習題請見本章應用練習 Part 11。

Chapter 4　應用練習

PART 1

請利用關係代名詞 who 或 whom 合併下列句子。不要用非正式的 who 來取代正式的 whom。

1. I have just written a thank-you note to Mr. Taylor. I stayed in his house during the floods.

   → _____

2. The person is a swindler. You bought some gold coins from him.

   → _____

3. The scream came from the child. His teeth were being examined by the dentist.

   → _____

4. Tell me about the little boy. His grandparents made him the heir to their fortune.

   → _____

5. This is the man. I gave your message to him.

   → _____

6. The manager is interviewing an applicant. He thinks she will be suitable for the job.

   → _____

7. I spoke to a girl about the activities of our club. Her name is Alison.

   → _____

8. Will you please call the girl? Her father has come to take her home.

   → _____

9. The motorist got into trouble with the traffic policeman. The motorist's license had not been renewed.

   → _____

10. The pilot of the helicopter was forced to make a landing. His arm was injured.

    → _____

11. The architect was congratulated. The architect's design has been approved.

    → _____

12. The person deserves his popularity. The person's life had been devoted to doing good.

    → _____

PART 2

請利用關係代名詞 whom 或 whose 合併下列句子。

1. Let me introduce you to the man. You admired his paintings so much.

   → _____

2. The children were enjoying themselves very much. We saw them at the beach.

→ _____

3. That is the nurse. We were telling you about her.

→ _____

4. Here come the boys. We have been waiting for them.

→ _____

5. You are the person. Everyone depends on you.

→ _____

6. I can't remember the fisherman. We borrowed his boat last summer.

→ _____

7. He is a man. His temper flares up easily.

→ _____

8. That is the team. We have to play against them in the finals.

→ _____

9. Those are the workers. Their salaries have been increased.

→ _____

10. Show me a photograph of the girl. You are corresponding with her.

→ _____

11. The boy has been elected chairman. His friends gave him much support.

→ _____

12. Where are the volunteers? You are looking for them.

→ _____

13. The shout came from the lady. Her house caught fire.

→ _____

14. Some of the swimmers did some fancy dives. We were watching them.

→ _____

15. I don't know the name of the boy. I borrowed the dictionary from him.

→ _____

16. A reporter was taking photographs of the girl. Her car was involved in the accident.

→ _____

17. Can you take me to the person? The order was issued by the person.

→ _____

基礎文法寶典 ❶
Essential English Usage & Grammar

18. The man glared at me. I accidentally stepped on his toes.

→ _____

19. He won't tell me the name of the man. He got the news through him.

→ _____

PART 3

請在空格中填入 who 或 whom 以完成句子。不要用非正式的 who 來取代正式的 whom。

1. The man _____ was nominated for the position declined it at the last minute.
2. The man _____ everyone is staring at is an actor.
3. The person _____ I want to see is not here.
4. Peter is the person _____ I feel is competent.
5. The man _____ drove the car was careless.
6. The student _____ has the largest collection of stamps will be awarded a prize.
7. The girl to _____ the letter was addressed had moved away several months ago.
8. My cousin _____ lives in Miami has entered the university there.
9. The man _____ coached the team was a former national player.
10. Mr. and Mrs. Gray were very interested in one of the children _____ lived in the orphanage.
11. The boy _____ I gave the money to just now has disappeared.
12. The driver _____ he employed is related to his gardener.

PART 4

請在空格中填入適當的關係代名詞 who、whom、whose、which 或 that 來完成句子。請注意 that 僅限用於一定要使用的情況，同時也避免用非正式的 who 來取代正式的 whom。

1. We are going to visit the lady _____ husband is the Assistant District Officer.
2. This is a picture of the man _____ we have been searching for since last week.
3. The present _____ he received from her was a silk shirt _____ she had bought in Misty Mountain.
4. The book from _____ I got this information belongs to Peter, _____ had received it as a birthday present from his cousin.
5. I visited my cousin _____ lives near the Skyline Caves.

6. The person _____ he once thought was his friend betrayed him.

7. The man _____ owns that stall is ill.

8. The girl _____ brother has just returned from Australia has invited me to her house.

9. The girl with _____ I was talking is my best friend.

10. He is the one _____ took the camera without their permission.

11. He is the man _____ patience I admire very much.

12. John Brown was the man _____ the manager said ought to have been promoted.

13. Have you found the person _____ you wanted to see?

14. The clerk from _____ I obtained the forms was very helpful.

15. The boy _____ told me that tale is Jennifer's brother.

16. During the holidays, I stayed with my uncle, _____ lives in Daisy Vale.

17. The girl _____ we were talking about last night has resigned.

18. The boy _____ saved the little girl from drowning was praised for his bravery.

PART 5

請利用關係代名詞 who、which 或 that 取代粗體字的部份來合併句子。請注意 that 僅限用於一定要使用的情況，同時也避免用非正式的 who 來取代正式的 whom。

1. The camera is made in Germany. He gave **it** to me for my birthday.

   → _____

2. Tell her about the snake. We killed **it** yesterday.

   → _____

3. The boys live next door. **They** took the apples.

   → _____

4. The person will get this album. **He** beats me at chess.

   → _____

5. The performance was very good. We saw **it** today.

   → _____

6. The postman is on leave. **He** usually brings our letters.

   → _____

7. He took the pills. **They** were strong enough to make him fall into a deep sleep.

   → _____

8. The army captain was a very brave man. **He** died in an accident on Saturday.

→ _____

9. Where is the pair of scissors? She lent **it** to you yesterday.

→ _____

10. We congratulated the student. **She** won a prize for good conduct.

→ _____

11. Mr. West is very proud of his antique telephone. He bought **the telephone** at an auction.

→ _____

12. The salesman is from our firm. **This salesman** sold you the vacuum cleaner.

→ _____

13. That is the best film. I have ever seen **the film**.

→ _____

14. Did you read in the newspapers about the boy? **This boy** helped the soldiers find a missing helicopter in the jungle.

→ _____

15. They are bringing some cakes. **The cakes** are very delicious.

→ _____

PART 6

請利用關係代名詞 who、whom、whose、which 或 that 取代粗體字的部份來合併句子。請注意 that 僅限用於一定要使用的情況，同時也避免用非正式的 who 來取代正式的 whom。

1. They found some golf balls. He lost **them** yesterday.

→ _____

2. We spoke to the lady. **She** sold the magazines to us.

→ _____

3. I have a friend. **His** brother works in the Customs Office.

→ _____

4. We went to a wedding. **The wedding** took place at the bride's house.

→ _____

5. Let me introduce you to the woman. **Her** daughter won first prize in the cooking contest.

→ _____

6. Peter is the boy. We all voted for **him**.

→ _____

7. The man is a plumber. **He** came to our house just now.

→ _____

8. The guests did not come. We invited **them** this morning.

→ _____

9. The bird is a wood pigeon. You saw **the bird** on the steps just now.

→ _____

10. I told him about the storm. **This storm** destroyed several houses last week.

→ _____

11. He kept a record of his employees. **These employees** were often late for work.

→ _____

12. The man was sick. We gave a glass of water to **him**.

→ _____

13. My friend has not returned the scooter yet. I lent it to **him** last night.

→ _____

14. The girl is blind and deaf. You saw **her** handiwork just now.

→ _____

15. They broke the promise. They made **the promise** before they left.

→ _____

PART 7

請利用關係代名詞 which 或 that 來合併句子。請注意 that 僅限用於一定要使用的情況。

1. This is the book. They quarreled over this book.

→ _____

2. He unwrapped the present. I had given him the present.

→ _____

3. That is the chair. He was sitting on that chair.

→ _____

4. There is a limit. Nobody can go beyond this limit.

→ _____

5. He will take you to the laboratory. They have spent a million dollars on the laboratory.

→ _____

6. The party will form the next government. The party obtains the most votes.

→ _____

7. I think this is the route. The hikers took this route.

→ _____

8. Have you found the key? Everybody is looking for the key.

→ _____

9. Mary explained the procedure to me. I was to follow the procedure.

→ _____

10. I am certain this is the diary. He writes down his appointments in the diary.

→ _____

11. The team will be declared the winner. The team scores the most points.

→ _____

12. He tried to brush off the ants. The ants were crawling all over his body.

→ _____

13. This is the tunnel. The train travels through it.

→ _____

14. She hung the clothes in the garden. She had washed the clothes earlier.

→ _____

15. This is the room. He keeps all his camera equipment in it.

→ _____

PART 8

請在空格中填入 who、whom、whose 或 which 來完成句子。不要用非正式的 who 來取代正式的 whom。

1. That boy over there, _____ father is a doctor, wants to be a doctor, too.

2. The children _____ you saw playing in the garden just now are my cousins, _____ have come here during their school holidays.

3. That girl, _____ sister is in my class, is a talented singer.

4. The prisoner, _____ I believe is innocent, is at present in jail.

5. My sister, _____ fiancé lives in Rainbow Valley, will be coming home soon.

6. My friend, _____ you spoke to last week, has gone overseas.

7. The University of Fairwinds, _____ has a large enrollment, is the first university established in the country.

8. Moon Island, _____ is located at the southern tip of the Long Peninsula, is a very popular holiday resort.

9. Mrs. Smith, _____ only son will be graduating from the university this year, is a widow.

10. Are tomatoes, _____ we are all fond of, classified as a vegetable or a fruit?

11. Charles, _____ lives on the outskirts of town, comes to school by bus.

12. Rose and Lily, _____ are twins, are studying in the same class.

13. My brother, _____ you saw last week, is flying to London today.

14. Abraham Lincoln, _____ became President of the United States, was born to a poor family.

15. His employer, to _____ he is very loyal, is a very pleasant and generous man.

16. My grandfather, _____ has a very long beard, prefers a pipe to cigarettes.

17. His pen pal, to _____ he writes frequently, lives in Holland.

18. The boys _____ helped raise funds for the society finally got to meet Mr. Johnson, _____ they had always admired.

PART 9

請利用非限定用法的關係代名詞 who、whom、whose 或 which 來合併句子。不要用非正式的 who 來取代正式的 whom。

1. The postman has been sent to the hospital. His leg was bitten by a mad dog.

→ _____

2. Irene recited a poem at the concert. Most people think she is a shy girl.

→ _____

3. Lauren lives nearby. I walked home with her last night.

→ _____

4. The girl wants the umbrella back now. You borrowed it from her yesterday.

→ _____

5. Mr. Smith is a well-known horse trainer. His horse just won the race.

→ _____

6. The man is my father. You saw him standing beside me yesterday.

→ _____

7. The artist has gone abroad. You admired his paintings at the exhibition.

→ _____

8. Mr. Gray is working in this bank. I introduced you to him last night.

→ _____

9. My uncle possesses a wonderful collection of coral. He lives near the sea on the East Coast.

→ _____

10. Benny has gone to the university to study law. He lived next door to me.

→ _____

11. Elephants are hunted by an increasing number of people. They are valued for their tusks.

→ _____

12. Paul has gone to America. His cousin is your neighbor.

→ _____

13. Betty would like to invite you to her party. You were introduced to her at Paul's house.

→ _____

14. Mr. Robinson will be coming here soon. I have great respect for him.

→ _____

15. My brother seems very pleased with you. I gave your message to him.

→ _____

16. Maria has been chosen as the winner of the essay competition. Her English is of a very high standard.

→ _____

17. The boys have decided not to go on the picnic. Their football match is on Saturday.

→ _____

18. Your friend has arrived with all his luggage. You are going with him to Happy Valley.

→ _____

PART 10

請利用非限定用法的關係代名詞 who、whom、whose 或 which 來合併句子。不要用非正式的 who

來取代正式的 whom。

1. Mr. Paul Jones is going to Canada next month. His brother is our neighbor.

    → _____

2. Mrs. Smith has to walk on crutches for a few days. She twisted her ankle yesterday.

    → _____

3. The man is waiting outside for you. I saw you talking to him this morning.

    → _____

4. Mr. Mason is very pleased and happy. His son won the prize for being the best student in his class.

    → _____

5. My brother will come home next week. He is studying in the United Kingdom.

    → _____

6. This supermarket belongs to Mr. Harrison. He is a very rich man.

    → _____

7. Jeanette has just come back. She went to Europe a year ago.

    → _____

8. That girl always comes to my house. Her brother is a friend of my brother's.

    → _____

9. Justin Reynolds is much admired. His ambition and personality made him the top man in the firm.

    → _____

10. Her younger brother saw the accident, too. He was with her.

    → _____

11. That team was expelled from the tournament. That team had broken the rules.

    → _____

12. He washed the glasses. It was all he would do for us.

    → _____

13. They changed all the locks in the house. It was a very wise thing to do.

    → _____

14. Mosquitoes breed very fast. They can be found in swampy areas.

    → _____

15. His friend accompanied him to the hospital. His friend's brother was a doctor.

→ _____

16. The man in front of me was talking very loudly. I do not know the man's name.

→ _____

17. Beethoven became deaf during his later years. His music is among the finest in the world.

→ _____

18. Mr. Cooper goes hunting whenever he can. His work confines him to the office.

→ _____

19. Madame Curie discovered radium. Her name is down in history as one of the greatest women of our age.

→ _____

PART 11

請利用正確的關係代名詞用法來合併句子。

1. I invited a few friends. One of them was my former classmate.

→ _____

2. He told me that only twenty persons passed the test. The majority of them were boys.

→ _____

3. We brought along some sandwiches. Most of them were eaten by Jim.

→ _____

4. They discovered an important letter. Parts of it were burned and charred.

→ _____

5. Fifteen people were believed to have been killed. Some of them were suspected to be children.

→ _____

6. They sent him many letters. He replied to only two of them.

→ _____

7. There were some guests staying at his house. One of them was an Australian.

→ _____

8. Eight people survived the crash. Three of them were members of the crew.

→ _____

9. There were some faint letters written on the wall. Two of the letters were distinguishable.

→ _____

10. In the desk was an old book. The cover of it was torn.

→ _____

11. He showed her some ladies' hats. None of them was to her liking.

→ _____

12. Mrs. Ford bought a scarf. The border of it was made of lace.

→ _____

13. More than sixty thousand came to watch the match. Many of them were from abroad.

→ _____

14. We wrote to about thirty people. Most of them never bothered to reply.

→ _____

15. Paul took part in many contests. A few of them were at an international level.

→ _____

16. Four other guys joined in at the last moment. One of them was a professor.

→ _____

17. There were only three Asians on the ship. Two of them were tourists.

→ _____

18. The bellboy brought in a large suitcase. The top of it was stamped with the names of various countries.

→ _____

19. He gained a lot of profit. Half of it was given to his partner.

→ _____

PART 12

請在空格中填入適當的關係代名詞來完成句子。請注意 that 僅限用於一定要使用的情況，同時也避免用非正式的 who 來取代正式的 whom。

1. The girl _____ had overheard the conversation told us what he had said about us.

2. Any newspaper _____ you read will give you the same news, though in a different style.

3. The child _____ toy was broken wanted his father to buy a new one for him.

4. The person _____ I just pointed out to you works in that office.

5. The man for _____ the police are looking has gone into hiding.

6. Is this the question _____ you wanted to ask me?

7. This is the wettest day _____ I have ever experienced.

8. All _____ the child wanted was a little love and kindness.

9. The person to _____ this novel is dedicated is the author's wife.

10. She wore the same wedding gown _____ her mother had worn at her own wedding twenty years ago.

PART 13

請利用關係代名詞 who、which 或 that 來合併句子。請注意 that 僅限用於一定要使用的情況。

1. She scolded the man. He stepped on her foot.

   → _____

2. I saw the carpet. You wanted to buy it.

   → _____

3. We met the salesman. He came to our house yesterday.

   → _____

4. These are the men. They rescued the children from the burning house.

   → _____

5. Can you show me the road? It leads to the railway station.

   → _____

6. The goat has been stolen. The goat was tied to the tree.

   → _____

7. She burned the letter. She received this morning.

   → _____

8. The boys need to be taught a lesson. They are in the other room.

   → _____

9. I'll invite my friends. They live opposite us.

   → _____

10. He threw away the shirt. It was torn.

   → _____

11. He killed the caterpillars. He found them on the leaves of his tree.

   → _____

12. My brother is to be discharged from the hospital soon. He fell from a ladder.

→ _____

13. There are several potholes in the road. It badly needs repairing.

→ _____

14. The guests have gone sightseeing. They arrived at the hotel this morning.

→ _____

15. The men have gone home for lunch. They work at the garage here.

→ _____

PART 14

請利用正確的關係代名詞用法來合併句子。請注意 that 僅限用於一定要使用的情況，同時也避免用非正式的 who 來取代正式的 whom。

1. Is that the boy? He saved the child from drowning.

→ _____

2. He asked me about the bicycle. He had left it outside the shed.

→ _____

3. She showed us the embroidery piece. She had been working on it the whole week.

→ _____

4. Do you know the contestant? He is wearing a red sweater.

→ _____

5. I closed the window. It was banging about in the wind.

→ _____

6. That car belongs to the man. He lives in that big house.

→ _____

7. We want to get tickets for the show. It starts at seven o'clock.

→ _____

8. There is something. I must tell you about it.

→ _____

9. The snake was identified as a viper. It bit the man.

→ _____

10. My brother pointed excitedly at the man. He had just boarded the bus.

→ _____

11. "Should I tell you about the stranger? He knocked at my door late one night."

→ _____

12. He pointed to the house. It was standing forlornly on the hilltop.

→ _____

13. The flats are to be pulled down. They were partly destroyed in the fire.

→ _____

14. The tie looks nice on him. He bought it in Hawaii.

→ _____

15. I saw two men. They were lurking suspiciously near the bushes.

→ _____

16. This is one of the things. Money cannot buy it.

→ _____

17. That is the boy. He kicked the ball through our window.

→ _____

PART 15

請利用正確的關係代名詞限定用法來合併句子。請注意 that 僅限用於一定要使用的情況，同時也避免用非正式的 who 來取代正式的 whom。

1. That is the hotel. My friend told me about it.

→ _____

2. The boy is a big bully. He lives next door.

→ _____

3. She threw away all the vegetables. They were turning bad.

→ _____

4. That is the boy. He saved me from drowning in that pool.

→ _____

5. He showed me the bicycle. His father had given it to him for his birthday.

→ _____

6. My mother threw away the box. It contained all my comics and storybooks.

→ _____

7. This is the first time. I have played volleyball.

→ _____

8. My parents have gone to see the house. The house had been put up for rent.

→ _____

9. Mary had a little lamb. It followed her to school every day.

→ _____

10. Many of the children went hunting for the treasure. Miss Brown had hidden it somewhere.

→ _____

11. The man must be brought to justice. He is responsible for this crime.

→ _____

12. She scolded the child for throwing stones at the dog. The dog belonged to the neighbors.

→ _____

13. The boy is going to be punished by the teacher. He stole the silver cup.

→ _____

14. The dog has been shot. It had bitten the little girl. She lives down the street.

→ _____

PART 16

請利用正確的關係代名詞限定用法來合併句子。請注意 that 僅限用於一定要使用的情況，同時也避免用非正式的 who 來取代正式的 whom。

1. Those are the people. Their homes were destroyed in the flood.

→ _____

2. You must meet Dr. Peters. I have already told you about him.

→ _____

3. Mary told us about her neighbor. His son had been killed in an accident.

→ _____

4. Many students are given free books and education. Their fathers are too poor to send them to school.

→ _____

5. They said that they were going to visit the old lady. Her daughter had just run away.

→ _____

6. Where is the girl? You were talking to her a few minutes ago.

   → _____

7. The man is waiting outside in his car. His daughter is in your class.

   → _____

8. Those children can go now. Their parents have arrived.

   → _____

9. The girl is talking to her friends in the garden. I borrowed the umbrella from her.

   → _____

PART 17

請利用正確的關係代名詞限定用法來合併句子。請注意 that 僅限用於一定要使用的情況，同時也避免用非正式的 who 來取代正式的 whom。

1. They went to see the old lady. Her son is a famous lawyer.

   → _____

2. He was riding his new bicycle. His uncle had given it to him for his birthday.

   → _____

3. She grew fond of the cat. She had found it on the way to school.

   → _____

4. The girl has to go home as soon as possible. I was talking to her a few minutes ago.

   → _____

5. Mrs. Black scolded the little boy. He had pulled her cat's tail.

   → _____

6. The books should be returned to the school library by tomorrow. They are on the table over there.

   → _____

7. All the children want to see this film. They like to watch Mickey Mouse.

   → _____

8. There are many people in the world today. They live only for pleasure and amusement.

   → _____

9. The bird is called a 'cockatoo.' You can see it in its cage near the door.

   → _____

10. The girl was wearing a beautiful, red dress with matching shoes and handbag. I passed her on the road just now.

   → _____

11. The suitcase is too expensive for me. I like it very much.

   → _____

12. The girl has been advised to make a report at the police station. Her bag had been stolen.

   → _____

13. I would like all of you to meet my cousin Belinda. She has come to my house for a short visit.

   → _____

PART 18

請利用正確的關係代名詞限定用法來合併句子。請注意 that 僅限用於一定要使用的情況，同時也避免用非正式的 who 來取代正式的 whom。

1. I heard a story. The story frightened me very much.

   → _____

2. That girl is very friendly. My sister is sharing a room with her.

   → _____

3. The spectators cheered loudly. They were watching the football match.

   → _____

4. The cat sleeps in that basket. It belongs to my youngest niece.

   → _____

5. Do you see the boy? We were talking about him yesterday.

   → _____

6. That girl works in my office. Her sister is a fashion designer.

   → _____

7. "Did I tell you about the stranger? I met him as I was walking home."

   → _____

8. The lady is my aunt. She is wearing a green dress.

   → _____

9. My brother brought home a basket of eggs. Half of them were rotten.

   → _____

10. The boys spent their holidays camping in Lighthouse Island. Five of them were scouts.

    → _____

11. He wrote to his friend. His friend was studying in London.

    → _____

12. That boy is my brother. Lucy is talking to him now.

    → _____

13. The cat is a Siamese cat. It is sleeping under the table.

    → _____

14. The meeting may be postponed. It was fixed for today.

    → _____

15. Our school team won the match. Two members of it are my classmates.

    → _____

16. My younger brother bought some goldfish. He kept them in a tank.

    → _____

17. Everyone mourned the death of that man. His acts of charity and generosity had made him popular.

    → _____

18. Aunt Mary sent the orphanage a box of old toys. Most of them were still in a very good condition.

    → _____

19. Henry wants to return the books. He borrowed them from you last month.

    → _____

20. The kittens cried pathetically. Their mother was dead.

    → _____

Chapter 5 連接詞

5-1 對等連接詞

> 對等連接詞 and、but、or、nor、for 或 so 等均可以用來連接文法結構對稱的單字、片語或子句。

(a) and 表示「附加」之意,中文常翻譯為「和、與」。

USAGE PRACTICE

▶ We bought a pair of shoes, a can of polish **and** a brush.

我們買了一雙鞋、一罐鞋油和一個刷子。

▶ We bought some apples **and** a bunch of grapes. 我們買了一些蘋果和一串葡萄。

▶ We brought oranges, bananas, apples, **and** grapes. 我們帶了柳丁、香蕉、蘋果和葡萄。

▶ There were two tables **and** a few chairs in the room. 房間裡有兩張桌子和幾張椅子。

▶ The lane was long **and** narrow. 這條巷子又長又窄。

▶ I was frightened **and** worried. 我很害怕也很擔心。

▶ It was cold **and** wet. 天氣又冷又濕。

▶ She burned the toast **and** spilled the coffee. 她把吐司烤焦,還把咖啡灑了出來。

▶ He turned away **and** pointed to the door. 他轉過身並指向大門。

▶ Go to her room **and** ask her to come here. 去她的房間,叫她來這裡。

 其他用來表示「附加」的連接詞性質用法還有 both...and(兩者都)、as well as(也)與 not only...but (also)(不僅…還…)等。

▶ I saw **both** Albert **and** Philip go into that shop. 我看見艾伯特和菲利浦走進那家店。

▶ The steps were narrow **as well as** steep. 這階梯又窄又陡。

▶ William, **as well as** his sister, plays the piano. 威廉和他的妹妹都彈鋼琴。

▶ She sings **not only** in English and French **but also** in Japanese.

她不只唱英文歌和法文歌,還唱日文歌。

▶ He is **not only** young **but also** impressionable. 他不但年輕而且容易受影響。

▶ **Not only** was the boy stupid, **but** he was stubborn. 這男孩不但愚蠢而且固執。

(b) but 可以表示「對比」或「不被預期的情況」,中文常翻譯為「但是、不過」。

USAGE PRACTICE

▶ The boy is intelligent **but** lazy. 這個男孩聰明，但是懶惰。

▶ He tried hard **but** lost. 他努力嘗試，但還是輸了。

▶ He looked at me **but** did not say anything. 他看著我，但是什麼話也沒説。

▶ I like to read, **but** he prefers to play games. 我喜歡閱讀，但是他比較喜歡玩遊戲。

▶ He may be naughty, **but** he is certainly endearing. 他也許頑皮，但他的確惹人喜愛。

▶ We did go there, **but** we didn't see him. 我們確實去過那裡，但是我們沒看到他。

▶ He hurt himself, **but** he did not cry. 他傷了自己，但是他沒哭。

▶ Joe is thin, **but** his brother is fat. 喬很瘦，但是他的弟弟很胖。

▶ I knocked at the door, **but** there was no answer. 我敲門，但沒有回應。

(c) or 表示「選擇」或「判斷」，中文常翻譯為「或者、否則」。

USAGE PRACTICE

▶ Does she prefer a red scarf **or** a white one? 她比較喜歡紅色的圍巾還是白色的？

▶ The town is twenty **or** twenty-five kilometers from here.

這小鎮距離這裡二十或二十五公里遠。

▶ Do you prefer tea **or** coffee? 你要茶還是咖啡？

▶ You can take it **or** leave it. 你可以拿走它或留下它。

▶ This musical box **or** that one is an appropriate gift for her.

這個音樂盒或那一個是適合送她的禮物。

▶ You mustn't take this route, **or** you'll find yourself far away from your cousin's house.

你絕對不可以走這條路線，否則你會發現自己遠離你堂哥的家。

 其他用來表示「選擇」或「判斷」的連接詞性質用法還有 either...or（兩者其一）、neither...nor（兩者皆非）等。當兩個主詞用 either...or 或 neither...nor 連接時，動詞要與比較靠近動詞的主詞一致。也可以單獨使用 nor 做連接，表示「也不」；nor 放在句首時，句子須倒裝。

▶ You can borrow **either** this book **or** that one. 你可以借這本書或那一本。

▶ I'll buy **either** this pair of shoes **or** that pair. 我會買這雙鞋或那雙。

▶ **Either** John **or** his friend must have left this wallet here.

一定是約翰或他的朋友把這皮夾留在這裡。

▶ She keeps her money **either** in the drawer **or** under her pillow.

她不是把她的錢放在抽屜裡就是她的枕頭下。

▶ You can write it **either** in your book **or** on a piece of paper. 你可以把它寫在你的書裡或一張紙上。

▶ **Either** you agree to my terms, **or** I won't sell it. 要嘛就是你接受我的條件，不然我不賣。

▶ **Either** you do this, **or** you resign your position. 你不是做這件事，就是離職。

▶ **Neither** Paul **nor** Mary has come here since last Friday.
從上星期五以來保羅和瑪麗都不曾來過這裡。

▶ We saw **neither** Richard **nor** his cousin at the station.
我們在車站既沒看到理查也沒看到他的表弟。

▶ She can wear **neither** this dress **nor** that one. 她不能穿這件洋裝也不能穿那一件。

▶ I know **neither** him **nor** his friend well. 我既不太認識他也不太認識他的朋友。

▶ He could **neither** sit **nor** sleep for three days. 他三天以來既不能坐下也不能睡覺。

▶ The stranger **neither** looked at **nor** spoke to anyone.
這個陌生人既不看任何人，也不跟任何人說話。

▶ **Either** Jenny **or** the children are at home. 不是珍妮就是孩子們在家。

▶ **Neither** Tom **nor** they have seen it. 湯姆和他們都不曾看見過它。

▶ **Neither** you **nor** I have been selected for the post. 你和我都沒被選上那職位。

▶ **Neither** Peggy **nor** her brother is willing to help. 佩姬和她弟弟都不願意幫忙。

▶ They cannot finish the work today, **nor** can they finish it tomorrow.
他們今天無法完成這個工作，明天他們也無法完成。

(d) for 可以連接表示「原因」的子句，表示此意時前面一般都會加上逗點，中文常翻譯為「因為」。

USAGE PRACTICE

▶ The construction workers had to stop working, **for** it was raining.
建築工人必須停止工作，因為正在下雨。

▶ I was very excited, **for** I was expecting a friend from Australia.
我很興奮，因為我在期待一個從澳洲來的朋友。

▶ She did not know anything, **for** I had not told her about it.
她什麼都不知道，因為我不曾把這件事告訴她。

▶ The beggar slept on the pavement, **for** he had no home.
這乞丐睡在人行道上，因為他沒有家。

(e) so 可以連接表示「結果」的子句，中文常翻譯為「所以」。

USAGE PRACTICE

▶ The door was not locked, **so** she was able to go in. 門沒鎖，所以她能進去。

▶ He insulted John, **so** John hit him in the jaw. 他侮辱約翰，因此約翰朝他的下巴打了一拳。

▶ We did not bring an umbrella, **so** we got wet. 我們沒帶雨傘，所以我們淋濕了。

▶ It was windy, **so** we stopped our badminton game. 風很強，所以我們停止羽球賽。

▶ We won the match, **so** we had a celebration. 我們贏得了比賽，所以我們辦了一個慶祝會。

▶ It was very noisy in the house, **so** I went out for a walk. 房子裡很吵，所以我出去散步。

▶ They had given me a ride, **so** I was very grateful to them.
他們曾載我一程，所以我很感激他們。

請在空格中填入適當的連接詞。

1. They told me that they might go to _____ the Grand _____ the Metro cinema.

2. He must have seen her _____ at Lucy's house _____ at her cousin's place.

3. _____ you pay him yourself _____ you give me the money and I'll pay him.

4. I did not see any of them: _____ Peter and Paul _____ Mary and Sally.

5. He was a complete failure; he succeeded _____ in his business _____ in his personal life.

6. _____ he _____ his wife knows anything about this. They were both out when it happened.

7. The car is cheap _____ economical to run.

8. I failed this time, _____ I'll try again and again until I succeed.

9. Mrs. Wilson is gentle _____ kind to everyone.

10. Lily _____ her younger sister are members of the Youth Club.

11. Our school team tried its best, _____ it was defeated.

12. Write to Uncle Bill _____ ask him when he is going overseas.

13. I have applied for many posts, _____ I have not once been successful.

14. In the box were bottled drinks, cakes, _____ fruit.

15. Both Jack _____ I had been asked to help, _____ we had to refuse.

16. The rooms were large _____ spacious, _____ they had a splendid view of the sea.

17. This shirt would cost only eight _____ nine dollars in Oakland.

18. He missed the bus, _____ he arrived late for the meeting.

19. Our destination was about thirty _____ forty kilometers to the north.

20. You must follow the instructions, _____ you won't get the experiment correct.

21. It was most fortunate that the lifeguard was there, _____ she would have drowned.

22. I'll take _____ you _____ your sister to the concert. I can't take both of you.

23. _____ Amy _____ Agnes wanted to go on a picnic with us, so we went without them.

24. _____ Sandra _____ Judy bothered to clean up the mess that they had made.

25. "Come on _____ Monday _____ Tuesday, and we'll have lunch together." "I'm afraid that _____ Monday _____ Tuesday is suitable for me."

26. You must be polite, _____ you'll get nowhere in your profession.

27. _____ Sam _____ his best friend did their homework; both of them were sent to detention class.

5-2 從屬連接詞

從屬連接詞 although、because、that、when、if 或 as 等可以用來引導表示「讓步」、「原因」、「結果」、「目的」、「時間」、「地點」、「條件」或「方式」等意義的副詞子句。

(a) 從屬連接詞 although/though（雖然）、even though（儘管）、even if（即使）或 however（無論）引導表示「讓步」的副詞子句，可置於主要子句的前面或後面。

USAGE PRACTICE

▶ **Although** it was raining, the sun was still shining. 雖然正在下雨，太陽依照耀著。

▶ **Although** they had lost the first match, they were not discouraged.
雖然他們輸掉了第一場比賽，但他們並不氣餒。

▶ **Although** we searched everywhere, we did not find it.
雖然我們到處都找遍，我們還是沒找到它。

▶ **Although** he studied hard, he failed. 雖然他用功唸書，但還是不及格。

▶ They joined the club **though** it was expensive. 雖然很貴，他們仍參加了這個俱樂部。

▶ **Though** she is her parents' favorite, she is not spoiled.

雖然她是她父母的最愛，但她並未被寵壞。

▶ **Even though** she was ill, she kept on working. 儘管她生病了，她仍繼續工作。

▶ She went on talking **even though** we were not listening.

儘管我們沒在聽，但她還是繼續講。

▶ **Even though** he was tired, he insisted on helping us.

儘管他累了，但他仍堅持要幫助我們。

▶ They did not believe her **even though** she answered very convincingly.

儘管她很有說服力地回答，他們還是不相信她。

▶ He has simple tastes **even though** he is a rich man. 儘管他是富豪，但他的品味很簡單。

▶ **Even if** you try your best, I don't think that you can do it.

即使你盡全力，我也不認為你能辦到。

▶ You've got to eat something **even if** you aren't hungry. 即使你不餓，你也得吃些東西。

▶ **However** difficult it is, you've got to try to do it. 無論這有多麼難，你都得試著做。

(b) 從屬連接詞 because、as 或 since 引導表示「原因」的副詞子句，常置於主要子句的後面（但也可以置於前面），中文常翻譯為「因為」。

USAGE PRACTICE

▶ We postponed the match **because** it was raining heavily. 因為下大雨，我們把比賽延期。

▶ He refused to speak **because** he had lost a tooth. 他因為掉了一顆牙而拒絕說話。

▶ We could not go that way **because** the road was blocked.

因為道路封閉，我們無法走那條路。

▶ We were surprised **because** she was so quiet during the party.

我們很驚訝，因為她在派對中是如此地安靜。

▶ He went home **because** there wasn't anything for him to do here.

因為他在這裡無事可做，他就回家去了。

▶ I like her **because** she is kind. 我喜歡她，因為她很親切。

▶ He cannot come **because** he has something else to do.

他不能來，因為他有其他的事情要做。

▶ **As** it was too heavy to carry, we left it at home. 因為它太重不便攜帶，我們把它留在家。

- She was disappointed **as** she had missed the film. 她很失望，因為她錯過了電影。
- **As** she was unwell, she did not go to school. 因為她不舒服，所以她沒去上學。
- She cannot wear the dress **as** it has shrunk. 她不能穿這件洋裝，因為它縮水了。
- We did not wait for him **since** he had told us he would be late.

  既然他已告訴我們他會遲到，我們就沒等他。
- He cannot read or write **since** he has never been to school.

  因為他從來沒上學過，他不會讀也不會寫。
- **Since** the place was in a mess, I had to tidy it up.

  因為這地方亂七八糟，所以我得把它整理乾淨。
- You will have to walk home **since** the last bus has already left.

  因為最後一班公車已經開走了，你將得走路回家。

(c) 從屬連接詞 so...that 或 such...that 引導表示「結果」的副詞子句，中文常翻譯為「以至於…」。

USAGE PRACTICE

- She was **so** angry **that** she scolded everyone. 她是如此氣憤以至於她責罵每個人。
- She was **so** happy **that** she cried. 她喜極而泣。
- The light was **such** a dazzling one **that** we were all blinded for a moment.

  這燈是如此耀眼，以至於我們全都暫時看不見。
- There was **such** an uproar **that** everyone woke up.

  有如此大的騷動以至於每個人都醒來了。

(d) 從屬連接詞 (so) that（以便…）、lest（唯恐）或 in order that（為了）引導表示「目的」的副詞子句。

USAGE PRACTICE

- She kept the door open **so that** they could go in when they liked.

  她讓門開著以便他們想進來就可以進來。
- She left the house early **so that** she could meet them at the station.

  她早早就離開家以便可以在車站和他們碰面。
- He took his raincoat **so that** he would not get wet if it rained.

他帶了他的雨衣以便在下雨時不被淋濕。

▶ She studies hard **so that** she can pass the exam. 她努力讀書以便能通過考試。

▶ I drew the curtains **so that** no light could enter. 我拉上窗簾以便不讓光線射進來。

▶ She squinted her eyes **so that** she could see better. 她瞇著眼以便看得更清楚。

▶ We took off our shoes **so that** we wouldn't make any noise.

我們把鞋子脫掉以便不發出噪音。

▶ My brother hitchhiked **so that** he might save some money.

為了能省些錢，我弟弟搭了便車。

▶ Write it down **lest** you forget. 唯恐你忘記，把它寫下來。

▶ The land was divided into equal plots **in order that** each person might get a fair share.

這土地被分為一樣大的小塊土地，為了讓每個人能夠等分。

(e) 從屬連接詞 when（當…時候）、as（在…之時）、while（在…發生的期間）、before（在…之前）、after（在…之後）、until/till（直到…）或 whenever（無論何時）引導表示「時間」的副詞子句。

USAGE PRACTICE

▶ **When** I came home, the door was open. 當我回到家時，門是開著的。

▶ **When** she saw the child fall, she ran forward to help him.

她看到那個小孩跌倒時，她跑上前去幫助他。

▶ They met with an accident **when** they were returning home. 他們正在回家時遭遇意外。

▶ **When** it was time for her to go on stage, she became nervous.

該她上舞台時，她變得緊張。

▶ **As** she was crossing the road, she found a bracelet. 當她在過馬路時，她發現一個手鐲。

▶ He shot the bird **as** it was flying. 當鳥在飛時，他射殺了牠。

▶ **As** we were walking down the street, we saw an accident.

當我們正沿著這條街走時，我們目睹一場意外。

▶ He bumped into a tree **as** he was cycling down the hill.

當他騎腳踏車下山丘時，他撞上一棵樹。

▶ **As** she was carrying the tray into the kitchen, she slipped and fell.

當她拿著托盤進廚房的時候，她滑了一跤而跌倒。

▶ **While** the teacher was talking, Victor was thinking of something else.

當老師在講話的時候，維克多正在想別的事情。

▶ Strike **while** the iron is hot. 打鐵要趁熱。

▶ Think carefully **before** you speak. 說話前要三思。

▶ Look **before** you leap. 三思而後行。

▶ Tory is allowed to play basketball **after** he has finished his homework.

托瑞做完功課後就可以去打籃球。

▶ **Whenever** he scores a goal, the crowd cheers. 每當他得分時，群眾就歡呼。

(f) 從屬連接詞 where（在…地方）或 wherever（無論何處）引導表示「地點」的副詞子句。

USAGE PRACTICE

▶ He forgot **where** he had left his book. 他忘記他把書遺留在何處。

▶ She takes her umbrella **wherever** she goes. 不論她到哪裡，都帶著傘。

▶ I'll follow you **wherever** you go. 無論你去哪裡，我都會跟隨你。

(g) 從屬連接詞 if（如果）、unless（除非）、as long as（只要）、provided that（在…條件下）、on condition that（在…情況下）或 supposing that（假設）引導表示「條件」的副詞子句。

USAGE PRACTICE

▶ Let me know **if** you are in trouble. 如果你有麻煩，就讓我知道。

▶ He will work for you **if** you pay him well. 如果你肯付他高薪，他會為你工作。

▶ You cannot drive a car **unless** you have a license.' 除非你有駕照，否則你不能開車。

▶ **Supposing that** he refuses to see you, what will you do? 假使他拒絕見你，你要怎麼辦？

(h) 從屬連接詞 as（以…方式）、as...as（和…一樣…）、so...as（和…一樣…）、as though/as if（好像）或 than（比…）引導表示「比較」或「方式」的副詞子句。

USAGE PRACTICE

▶ A disobedient child never does **as** he is told. 叛逆的孩子從不做別人要他做的事。

▶ I will spend my money **as** I please. 我要隨我喜歡地花錢。

▶ I can run **as** fast **as** you can. 我能跑得和你一樣快。

▶ I cannot run **so** fast **as** you. 我無法跑得和你一樣快。

▶ I cannot type **so** well **as** that typist. 我打字無法像那位打字員一樣好。

▶ She behaved **as though** she were a queen. 她表現得好像她是個皇后。

▶ He was treated **as if** he were an animal. 他被像動物一般地對待。

▶ He acted **as if** he had seen an apparition. 他的樣子看起來好像見鬼了。

▶ This exercise is more difficult **than** I thought. 這練習比我想像中還困難。

請在空格中填入適當的連接詞。

1. He makes friends _____ he goes.

2. I will not give you permission _____ you do _____ I say.

3. He can run _____ fast _____ I can.

4. I am not sure _____ my friend lives _____ _____ she took me to her home last week.

5. She cannot play the piano _____ well _____ I can _____ she began her lessons earlier.

6. You have changed a lot _____ I last saw you; in fact, more _____ I thought a person could ever change.

7. The men were treated _____ _____ they were criminals _____ they had not committed any crime.

8. _____ they saw the bull charging at them, they ran _____ fast _____ they could; they hardly knew _____ they were heading.

9. Despite the fact that I could not type _____ well _____ she could, I managed to finish my work sooner _____ she did.

10. _____ you need my help with mathematics, just let me know. I may be able to help _____ _____ I may not excel in it.

11. "Hand out your books _____ you go home," the teacher said. "Remember that I will not mark them _____ you have completed the exercises."

12. _____ she is rich, she lives frugally, saving a few cents _____ she can.

13. She always does _____ she is told, _____ _____ she goes against her own principles.

14. You must always strike _____ the iron is hot; _____ you strike too early or too late it is _____ _____ you have not done anything at all.

15. _____ _____ she is poor, she helps anyone _____ she can with the little she has.

16. No one knew _____ it had come from _____ it had been with them for a long time.

☞ 更多相關習題請見本章應用練習 Part 1。

5-3 準連接詞

準連接詞雖然實際上是副詞，但同時具有連接詞的功用，可以用來表達前後句子之間的邏輯關係。請注意，除了 yet 和 or else 之外，其他準連接詞要連接句子時，前面要有另外的連接詞或是使用分號，後面則通常接逗點與句子隔開。

(a) 準連接詞 yet、still、however 或 nevertheless 引導表示「對比」的副詞子句，作「但是、然而」解。

USAGE PRACTICE

▶ The old man is weak, **yet** he does strenuous work. 這老人很虛弱，但他仍做粗重的工作。

▶ He was hungry, **yet** he did not feel like eating. 他餓了，但他不想吃東西。

▶ She is ill; **still**, she refuses to see a doctor. 她生病了，但是她拒絕去看醫生。

▶ I warned him about the danger; **still**, he insists on going.
我警告他危險，但他還是堅持要去。

▶ I have failed; **however**, I will try again. 我失敗了；然而，我會再試一次。

▶ The boat was ancient; **however/nevertheless**, it was in good condition.
這船很老舊；然而，它的狀況良好。

▶ Their teacher is strict; **nevertheless**, they like her.
他們的老師很嚴格；然而，他們很喜歡她。

(b) 準連接詞 besides、moreover、furthermore 或 also 引導表示「附加說明」的副詞子句，作「此外、而且、再者」解。

▶ The dress was beautiful; **furthermore**, it was well-tailored.

這洋裝很漂亮；此外，它剪裁得很好。

▶ The old man was always jovial; **besides**, he was very kind.

老人總是很愉快；而且，他很仁慈。

(c) 準連接詞 therefore、thus、hence、accordingly 或 consequently 引導表示「結果」或「後果」的副詞子句，作「因此、所以」解。

▶ He has done something wrong; **therefore**, he must be punished.

他做錯事，因此他必須受罰。

▶ He committed the crime; **hence** he was jailed. 他犯了罪，因此他被監禁。

▶ Andrew caught the robbers; **thus** he was commended.

安德魯抓到那些強盜，因此他受到讚揚。

▶ They broke the glass window; **accordingly**, they had to pay for it.

他們打破了玻璃窗，因此他們得付錢賠償。

▶ He broke many school rules; **consequently**, he was expelled.

他違反許多校規，因此他被退學。

(d) 表示「否則」的準連接詞有 or else 和 otherwise。

▶ I had to tell them **or else** they would have hurt me.

我得告訴他們，否則他們會傷害我。

▶ We had to do something fast **or else** she would have fallen.

我們得趕緊行動，否則她會跌倒。

▶ You must help us; **otherwise**, we will inform the police about your crimes.

你必須幫助我們；否則我們會向警察揭發你的罪行。

Chapter 5　應用練習

PART 1

請在空格中填入適當的連接詞。

1. I will report your dog to the police _____ you don't chain him up.

2. Michael is lame but he can run _____ fast _____ I can.

3. I cannot write _____ beautifully _____ you do.

4. He met a group of friends _____ he was cycling home.

5. I can't use that machine _____ it is in need of repair.

6. He acts _____ _____ he were the chairman of the board.

7. The prisoners were treated _____ _____ they were animals.

8. _____ he was asleep, I tiptoed out of the room.

9. I will go _____ I like and _____ you try to stop me, I'll never forgive you!

10. I cannot throw the javelin _____ far _____ Felix can _____ I am stronger than he is.

11. _____ _____ she works hard, her stepfather is never satisfied.

12. The doctor said, "I'll come _____ soon _____ I can. Don't touch the injured man _____ he is in an awkward position."

13. The lion is roaring with pain _____ its foot is trapped in a snare. _____ hard it tries, it can't shake off the trap.

14. _____ he is the youngest child in the family, he is not _____ spoiled _____ his brothers.

15. "_____ you come any nearer, I'll call the police!" the girl cried.

PART 2

請在空格中填入適當的連接詞。

1. They spent the night here _____ it was too late for them to go home.

2. I cannot afford to buy this watch _____ I like it very much.

3. She said that she can't come _____ she has a lot of work to do.

4. You must shut all the windows _____ _____ the rain will not come in.

5. I returned the book to him _____ came back at once.

6. The front door was locked, _____ I went around the house to the back door.

7. I could not sleep at all _____ the neighbor's cat was mewing the whole night long.

8. _____ _____ I had dressed as quickly as I could, I missed the bus.

9. He was very wealthy, _____ he was also one of the most miserly men I had ever known.

10. You can _____ use my bicycle _____ walk up the hill.

11. They have stopped the game _____ it has started raining rather heavily.

12. I have not seen your purse anywhere, _____ have I taken it.

13. I read through the whole book, _____ I could not get the information I wanted.

14. _____ he was very busy, he offered to help me _____ I did not know anything about the subject.

15. I went to his house yesterday, _____ he was not in.

16. _____ they were very expensive, we decided to take them.

PART 3

請在空格中填入適當的連接詞。

1. He has a broad face _____ tiny eyes.

2. _____ _____ she was tired, she continued to work.

3. John _____ Mary like swimming.

4. He armed himself with a fishing rod _____ went to the lake.

5. They had bread _____ coffee, _____ they had no butter.

6. He made a resolution not to smoke, _____ he did not keep it.

7. The trade fair was not a success, _____ no one made any profit.

8. He shouted with all his strength, _____ no one answered.

9. _____ the servant washed the dishes _____ swept the floor, she did not wipe off the stove.

10. The ship ran into a storm _____ was wrecked. Some of the passengers were rescued _____ many died.

11. The prizes included a refrigerator _____ a television set. No one won _____ many tried.

12. She soaked the clothes _____ left them overnight.

13. _____ he had prepared the speech, he did not tell anyone about it.

14. He ate the rice _____ the curry, _____ he did not touch the vegetables _____ he used to like them very much.

15. _____ he is short, he is a good volleyball player.

16. We had to suspend the game _____ _____ the players would have got hurt in such a bad weather.

17. There was _____ a fuss over the missing letter _____ even detectives were employed to investigate into the matter.

PART 4

請在空格中填入適當的連接詞。

1. He got up early _____ he could not sleep.

2. Don't litter the place, _____ you will be fined.

3. _____ you _____ Rosie must have borrowed it.

4. Many people dream of becoming rich _____ famous, _____ very few realize their dreams.

5. He had the choice of _____ going to the university _____ becoming a businessman.

6. The two brothers went fishing in the lake _____ did not catch any fish.

7. _____ Eddie _____ Nick was absent from school yesterday. They were both present.

8. He did not take the white shirt _____ the blue one.

9. She took with her a bag containing her swimsuit _____ a towel _____ she was going swimming in the nearby pool.

10. He lost the game, _____ he did not lose his temper _____ he had every reason to.

11. You can have some sausages _____ some bacon, _____ you can't have both.

12. She did not agree to do it _____ Paul _____ John were going to help her.

13. The weather was bright _____ clear, _____ no one was on the beach because of the early hour.

14. We did not borrow his drawing board _____ his brushes _____ we knew he needed them.

15. The girls were not allowed to wear makeup _____ high-heeled shoes to school.

16. _____ the car was an old model, it was still in excellent condition.

PART 5

請在空格中填入適當的連接詞。

1. We will have to wait for the next bus _____ the three o'clock one has just passed.

2. The roof is still leaking _____ it was mended yesterday.

3. You may borrow _____ this book _____ that one, _____ you can't have both of them.

4. John _____ Michael will enter the university this year, _____ _____ both of them want to start working.

5. That man was sent to prison for life _____ he had murdered his wife.

6. The little girl fell down the stairs _____ hurt herself.

7. _____ she was not seriously hurt, she cried loudly.

8. _____ Tony _____ his brother played in the match last week _____ both of them were down with a fever.

9. She cannot cook _____ sew, _____ she is an expert in flower arranging.

10. An oil company announced that it had discovered oil in that area, _____ it was later discovered to be a hoax.

11. He was dismissed from the company _____ he was late for work every morning _____ refused to try to be on time.

12. She went to the chemist _____ bought a bottle of suntan lotion _____ she was going to the beach.

13. The customer complained loudly about his food _____ it tasted too salty.

14. He did not sign _____ this document _____ that one.

15. The car refused to move _____ the engine had gone cold. He took off his shirt _____ began to push the car.

PART 6

請在空格中填入適當的連接詞。

1. The visitors arrived _____ she was preparing dinner.

2. She was crying bitterly, _____ I asked her what the matter was.

3. _____ I go home, I'll read up on this subject.

4. _____ I was too ill to go, she offered to go in my place.

5. I read through the book _____ _____ I could get some information on the life of Alexander the Great.

6. _____ _____ there weren't many people at the party, it was a most enjoyable occasion.

7. We went to the seaside _____ enjoyed ourselves very much.

8. She should wear _____ her new blue dress _____ the white lace one to the party.

9. _____ he had promised to come home early, he returned late _____ made Mother angry.

10. Don't expect him to come; he has _____ the time _____ the money to make the trip.

11. _____ we last saw him, he was in good health. It is a shock to hear of his death.

12. _____ we were returning home, we found that one of the boys was missing, _____ we turned back to search for him.

13. He thought his parents would be home late, _____ he made a feast for himself with all the food in the house.

14. _____ they entered the house, they found that it had been ransacked. _____ _____ nothing was missing, they called the police _____ reported the case.

15. He could not go _____ he was ill _____ the doctor had advised him to stay in bed. He had missed the excursion, _____ he did not feel too disappointed.

16. He worked as quickly as he could _____ _____ he would be in time for his favorite television program.

PART 7

請在空格中填入適當的連接詞。

1. I looked into the room, _____ it was too dark to see anything.

2. The man said that he would come the next day, _____ he was right on time.

3. He may be a very clever boy, _____ that doesn't mean he doesn't need to work hard.

4. _____ it was raining very heavily, he insisted on going out with his friend.

5. _____ _____ the rock was very heavy, we managed to push it off the road.

6. It started to drizzle, _____ the boys continued with the football game.

7. I kept as quiet and still as possible _____ _____ my nose was beginning to itch.

8. I gave him the letter _____ told him to post it.

9. I haven't forgotten her at all _____ she doesn't even remember my name.

10. The man unlocked the drawer _____ took out a loaded revolver.

11. He was all alone in the forest, _____ he wasn't frightened at all.

12. I could not reach the can of cookies on the shelf _____ _____ I was standing on a chair.

13. She gave me the book _____ left at once, saying that she was in a hurry to get home.

14. We were waiting for them the whole day, _____ they didn't turn up.

15. The thieves broke the lock _____ entered the house, _____ they did not find anything valuable.

16. _____ _____ he is only a child, he is very intelligent _____ can solve very difficult problems within a few minutes.

17. I stopped her on the road _____ questioned her, _____ she denied knowing anything about it.

18. The thief managed to escape from the police _____ fled to a hideout near the jungle, _____ the police followed his trail _____ caught him after a brief gunfight.

PART 8

請在空格中填入適當的連接詞或準連接詞。

1. She could not afford to buy that doll _____ _____ she liked it very much, _____ she bought the other one instead.

2. I did not borrow your pen, _____ have I seen it around. Perhaps you had dropped it _____ you were running home.

3. The road was winding _____ _____ _____ steep, _____ we had to drive slowly all the way.

4. Steven was a strong swimmer, _____ he failed to win the race.

5. The walls of the hut were falling apart; m_____, the roof was leaking in many places.

6. Do you want to come with us _____ stay at home? You must make up your mind _____ _____ I can arrange things.

7. _____ he came home, he found two letters _____ a parcel on the table for him.

8. Paul _____ Tony came to visit me yesterday, _____ I was not at home. T_____, they left a message.

9. The night was not cold, _____ he was shivering.

10. She did not attend the wedding dinner _____ she had a bad cold _____ preferred to

rest in bed.

11. The lighting in his room was poor; t_____ , he suffered from eye weakness.

12. _____ Terry _____ his sister can come with me in my car _____ _____ it will be less packed in the other car.

13. The sampan was small; s_____ , it shot ahead of all the other boats in the race.

14. _____ Sammy fell off his bicycle, he did not cry _____ _____ his knees were hurt.

15. _____ it looked like rain, we postponed our trip to another day.

16. _____ it was quite late, she did not go to sleep _____ continued writing the essay _____ it had to be passed in the next day.

17. The plant died _____ you did not look after it well. A_____ , it was not suited to the conditions here.

18. He woke up late, _____ he had to hurry through his breakfast _____ _____ he wouldn't miss the bus.

19. Tony is blind; n_____ , he is the most cheerful person in the center.

PART 9

請在空格中填入適當的連接詞或準連接詞。

1. He was old _____ weak, _____ there was no one to look after him.

2. My mother gave me _____ _____ a birthday present _____ _____ some money _____ _____ I could buy myself a new dress.

3. _____ we found that we might be late, we took a taxi _____ _____ we might reach the movie theater on time.

4. That old man had expected free treatment _____ he was poor. H_____ , he was shocked when he was given a bill for thirty dollars.

5. You'd better work hard _____ _____ you'll fail.

6. Mona, _____ _____ _____ her sister, is in the choir.

7. You can _____ ride the motorcycle _____ drive the car. H_____ , you'd better take the motorcycle _____ part of the road is blocked.

8. _____ the escaped convict _____ his accomplice darted into a house to escape the police, the effort was wasted. The police _____ their dogs surrounded the house

immediately.

9. _____ my cousin _____ his friend cannot come early _____ they are busy doing their work, _____ they promise to come as soon as they can.

10. Our feast included food and drinks. There was a large quantity of each; s_____ , we managed to finish them.

11. The teacher had punished them _____ _____ _____ they might learn to do their work properly. N_____ , they still produced the same careless work.

12. The girls practiced hard, _____ they did not win the match; h_____ we cheered them _____ they showed a fine spirit of sportsmanship.

13. My mother _____ my father visited my uncle _____ aunt in England. My parents traveled by air _____ they wanted to arrive early, _____ instead they were a few hours late.

14. The teacher told that boy _____ his friends to _____ follow the rules _____ be sent to detention class.

15. The girl is young _____ poor, _____ she earns her own living by weaving baskets _____ sewing dresses.

PART 10

請在不改變句意的原則下，用適當的連接詞合併句子。

1. We were watching television. All the lights went off.

    → _____

2. I was afraid. I did not show it.

    → _____

3. They started early. They could reach the station on time.

    → _____

4. It was not very dark. He switched on the light.

    → _____

5. They are blind. They can do a lot of things.

    → _____

6. We waited for another half hour. He did not appear.

    → _____

7. There was a slight drizzle. Many people came to watch the game.

→ _____

8. I tied up the boat. It wouldn't drift away.

→ _____

9. His mother was in the kitchen. He slipped in unnoticed.

→ _____

10. They refused to tell me. I could guess what was going on.

→ _____

11. The jungle was dense with undergrowth. We managed to cut our way through.

→ _____

12. She was stepping off the bus. It started to move.

→ _____

13. She searched all over the house. She couldn't find the letter.

→ _____

14. I left a light on. The house wouldn't be in complete darkness.

→ _____

15. The club members were leaving the room. The chairman called out to them.

→ _____

16. I warned Alex not to interfere in their business. He insists on doing so.

→ _____

17. Their school team had lost the match. They were not discouraged. They congratulated us.

→ _____

18. It was dinner time. Pauline was not hungry.

→ _____

19. I was on the bus. I saw Ben crossing the road. He did not see me.

→ _____

20. She wanted to leave without wasting time. She sat down to write a note to her uncle. He wouldn't worry about her.

→ _____

PART 11

請在不改變句意的原則下，用適當的連接詞合併句子。

1. I did not hear him come in. I was thinking about my work.

   → _____

2. There was so much noise. I could hardly hear him.

   → _____

3. They did the work as fast as possible. They could go home in time for tea.

   → _____

4. My friends didn't come to my house. They were too busy with the arrangements.

   → _____

5. I wanted to go over to Sandra's house. I could meet Michael and James there.

   → _____

6. She was writing a letter to her pen pal. She suddenly heard a loud crash.

   → _____

7. She ran to the door quickly. She thought someone had fallen down the stairs.

   → _____

8. I was watching her closely. I saw her take something from Peter's wallet.

   → _____

9. They put away their books and went out to play. It was already four o'clock.

   → _____

10. She copied down the poem. She could read it to her younger sister.

    → _____

11. The room looked drab. We cut some flowers and placed them in a vase on the table.

    → _____

12. She was very angry with me. She thought that I had pulled her hair in class.

    → _____

13. The old man tended the orchids carefully. He wanted to win a prize in the Flower Show.

    → _____

14. The servant was ironing some shirts. She heard a loud scream for help.

    → _____

PART 12

請在不改變句意的原則下，用適當的連接詞合併句子。

1. She was ill. She did not go to the office. She went to see a doctor.

   → _____

2. He ran fast. He wanted to catch the train.

   → _____

3. She washed the clothes. She hung them out to dry. She took them back again. She saw dark clouds gathering in the sky.

   → _____

4. I have not seen your book. I have not borrowed it.

   → _____

5. He did not want to go home. He had done something very wrong.

   → _____

6. The wind was strong. Rain fell heavily. We managed to come.

   → _____

7. That boy did not complete his work. He was lazy. The teacher punished him.

   → _____

8. You must hurry up. You will be late for school.

   → _____

9. The river was flooded. The roads were flooded, too. It had been raining for many days.

   → _____

10. Pauline ran fast. Margaret ran fast, too. Jane ran faster.

    → _____

11. The two men were weary. They were thirsty. They had walked under the hot desert sun for a long time.

    → _____

12. The flood was over. People returned to their homes. They found that everything had been destroyed.

    → _____

13. Peter did not see it. Thomas did not see it. There must be someone who had seen it.

    → _____

14. That girl speaks English. She also speaks many other foreign languages. She is an outstanding

基礎文法寶典 ❶
Essential English Usage & Grammar

student.

→ _____

15. We must do something quickly. She will fall into the river.

→ _____

16. She reads fast. I can never read so fast.

→ _____

PART 13

請在不改變句意的原則下，用適當的連接詞合併句子。

1. He tried to stop the car. He saw the boy running across the road.

→ _____

2. I did not see your kitten. I heard a kitten crying in my backyard.

→ _____

3. You must water those plants. They will wither. They will die.

→ _____

4. He stepped out of his house. He went in again. He saw dark clouds gathering in the sky.

→ _____

5. Robert can carve well. His brother can also carve well.

→ _____

6. He likes to watch people swimming. He has never tried to swim before. He is afraid of water.

→ _____

7. He is a wealthy man. He has very simple tastes. He is generous to the needy, too.

→ _____

8. Linda can run fast. I can run fast too. I did not win a prize.

→ _____

9. The cost of making a cement badminton court here can run up to two thousand dollars. It can also run up to three thousand dollars.

→ _____

10. He finished reading the letter. He felt very angry. He burned the letter.

→ _____

11. He lost his watch. He dared not go home. His parents would scold him.

→ _____

12. Mr. Jackson was very happy. He had won first prize in the lottery. He hadn't received his money yet. He gave his friends a big dinner.

→ _____

13. The fire had died down. They tried to salvage whatever they could find.

→ _____

14. The woman is very old. She is strong.

→ _____

PART 14

請在不改變句意的原則下，用適當的連接詞合併句子。

1. He took careful aim with his pistol. He missed the target.

→ _____

2. The river burst its banks. It flooded the whole town.

→ _____

3. Ben did not switch on the fan. He felt very hot.

→ _____

4. The scouts soon had their tents set up. They had the fire lighted, too.

→ _____

5. She cooked the vegetables. She fried the fish. She did not cook the meat.

→ _____

6. He lighted his cigarette. He threw the match on the floor.

→ _____

7. There were two letters on the table. There were three cards, too.

→ _____

8. The man was caught. He was sentenced to life imprisonment.

→ _____

9. His family was poor. He had never borrowed from anyone.

→ _____

10. He tried very hard. He failed the examination.

→ _____

11. They were hungry. They did not eat much at dinner.

→ _____

12. This man is deaf. He is dumb. He has a good job.

→ _____

13. He fell from a tree. He broke his left leg.

→ _____

PART 15

請在不改變句意的原則下，用適當的連接詞合併句子。

1. Robin bought the shirt. He liked it.

→ _____

2. It was raining hard. They had to stay indoors.

→ _____

3. The tunnel was dark. It was narrow, too.

→ _____

4. Their car ran out of gas. They had to walk to the nearest village to get some.

→ _____

5. There was no electricity in the village. There was no proper water supply, either.

→ _____

6. Do you sleep in this room? Do you sleep in the other room?

→ _____

7. The journey was slow. One of the scouts had twisted his ankle.

→ _____

8. I have not taken your book. I have not seen it anywhere.

→ _____

9. She took a pair of scissors. She cut the string in two.

→ _____

10. The man refused to ferry us across. The river was too swift and dangerous.

→ _____

11. The door was left slightly open. I could hear every word they said.

→ _____

12. The hawk swooped down. It snatched the chicken away.

    → _____

13. You can pass in your book today. You can pass it in tomorrow.

    → _____

14. All of us were tired. We were hungry, too.

    → _____

15. He was tied securely. He could not move. He could not call out.

    → _____

16. Mr. Mason broke a traffic law. He had to pay a fine. He had to be imprisoned for one month.

    → _____

PART 16

請在不改變句意的原則下，用適當的準連接詞改寫句子。

1. He needs a haircut badly. The barber shop is closed today.

    → _____

2. A fishbone was stuck in her throat. She couldn't swallow her food.

    → _____

3. They were very tired after their long climb uphill. They walked to the tree. They sat down under it.

    → _____

4. He was very busy. He found time to write to his parents.

    → _____

5. She bought a box of soap powder from the salesman. He refused to leave. He wanted her to buy something else.

    → _____

6. It was raining. We decided to go.

    → _____

7. Tony swam very well. He did not win the competition.

    → _____

8. You can choose this puppy. You can choose that puppy. You cannot have both of them.

    → _____

PART 17

請在不改變句意的原則下，用適當的連接詞合併句子。

1. I used torchlight. It was very dark by then.

   → _____

2. I wanted to go with them very badly. My father would not let me go.

   → _____

3. I went to see the manager personally. I had a very serious complaint to make.

   → _____

4. The bull rushed straight at the little boy. He quickly moved to another side.

   → _____

5. I locked myself in my bedroom. I would not be disturbed by the children.

   → _____

6. We had waited for you for a long time. You did not turn up at all.

   → _____

7. He was very pleased with himself. He had won first prize in the competition.

   → _____

8. The girl did not buy that expensive pair of shoes. She liked them very much.

   → _____

9. He walked out of the room very angrily. He slammed the door hard.

   → _____

10. I shouted for help as loudly as I could. No one heard me.

    → _____

11. You must come early. We will have time to make all the arrangements.

    → _____

12. I did not steal the pears from your orchard. My brother did not steal them, either.

    → _____

13. I could not find him in his own house. I went over to Alex's house to see if he was there.

    → _____

14. We were walking to the other side of the island. We found a small stream.

    → _____

基礎文法寶典 ❶
Essential English Usage & Grammar

習 題 解 答

Chapter 1 解答

1–1 小練習

1. a　2. a　3. an　4. an　5. a　6. an　7. a　8. a　9. an　10. a　11. a　12. an　13. a

14. an　15. an　16. a　17. an　18. an　19. a　20. a　21. an　22. an　23. an　24. an　25. a　26. a

應用練習

PART 1

1. a/the　2. an/the　3. a/the　4. ✕　5. the　6. the　7. an/the　8. a/the　9. ✕　10. the　11. a

12. ✕　13. the　14. a/the　15. the　16. a　17. a/the　18. the　19. an/the　20. ✕　21. ✕　22. the

23. ✕　24. ✕　25. a/the　26. the　27. the　28. an　29. ✕　30. a/the

PART 2

1. ✕; an　2. the; an; the　3. The; the; the　4. An; The; the　5. a; the　6. The; The

7. a; ✕　8. the; the; the　9. a; ✕; ✕; ✕; the　10. a; an　11. the; the; the; the/a　12. a; the; the

13. the; ✕　14. The; the; a

PART 3

1. the; the　2. ✕; ✕　3. a; the　4. a; an　5. ✕; a; the　6. ✕; the; the; ✕; a　7. A; a; an; ✕

8. the; an; the　9. ✕; an　10. A; A; ✕; an; a　11. The; the; the; the　12. the; the; the; ✕

13. An; a; the; ✕

PART 4

1. the; ✕　2. the; ✕; the; the; the　3. the; the; the　4. An; an; A　5. ✕; an; The; a

6. The; ✕; the　7. A; a; a; a　8. an; the　9. an; a　10. an; the; ✕; the　11. a; ✕; a; a

12. the/a; an; a　13. a; a; the; an; a　14. An; an; the　15. The; ✕; ✕; the

PART 5

1. an; the; a; a; the　2. An; ✕; a; A; an　3. An; a; a; the　4. ✕; ✕; ✕; ✕; ✕; A; ✕

5. The; a; a; ✕; ✕; ✕　6. a; the; ✕; the; the　7. An/The; the; the; A; a; The; an; the

8. The; a; the; ✕　9. an; the; the　10. ✕; ✕　11. The; ✕; The; the　12. The; a; the; the

13. a; the; a; the; the　14. A/✕; the; the; the; The　15. ✕; The; a　16. the/a; The; ✕; the/a

17. The; a; the　18. The; a; the; The; ✕

PART 6

1. a; the; The; the; the　2. a; the　3. The; the; the　4. The; the　5. a; the; the; the

6. an/the; a; the　7. The; the　8. ✕; a/✕; an; the　9. The; ✕; the; ✕; a; ✕　10. the

11. The; a; ×; the   12. the; the; ×; ×   13. a; a; a   14. the; the; an   15. the; the; ×

PART 7

1. the; an; a; the   2. a; the; the; ×   3. A/the; the; the   4. a; ×; the; the; an   5. The; ×; the; a; an

6. an; the; an; the; a; a   7. The; a; the; ×   8. the; a; the; an; the; the   9. ×; an; a; the; an

10. A; the; An; a; an; the   11. a; a; an; a; the   12. The; the; the; the/×; the; the; a; an; the

13. a; ×; ×; the; The; a; the; the; the   14. a; a; an; an; a; a; a; the; the; the; ×

Chapter 2　解答

2-1 小練習

1. the monkeys' tails   2. the foot of the mountain   3. Francis' new car   4. the eye of the needle

5. a minute's pause   6. the movement of the earth   7. her brother-in-law's car

8. the results of the examination   9. wolves' howling   10. Ari's message

11. the heiress'/heiress's jewels   12. the judge's decision   13. the end of the line

14. the chairman's speech   15. the twinkling of the stars   16. the secretary's salary

17. the tourists' luggage   18. the source of the river   19. my niece's toys   20. two months' absence

21. the policemen's hats   22. the colors of the flowers   23. the position of London   24. the bees' stings

25. the sides of the box   26. the body's needs   27. the moon's surface   28. the rim of the jug

29. the workers' union   30. two dollars' worth

2-2 小練習

1. shelves   2. cliffs   3. lives   4. safes   5. trout   6. cod   7. loaves   8. oases

9. information   10. oxen   11. bamboos   12. Chinese   13. bases   14. spies   15. children

16. witches   17. sheep   18. staff   19. ovens   20. advice   21. bread   22. handkerchiefs

23. formulas/formulae   24. phenomena   25. daughters-in-law

2-3 小練習

1. hardship   2. absentee   3. government/governess/governor   4. development/developer

5. mentality   6. competition/competitor   7. revision   8. width   9. richness   10. pride

11. youth   12. truth   13. length   14. timidity   15. highness/height   16. obligation   17. vanity

18. brutality   19. suddenness   20. realism/realist/reality   21. anxiety   22. perfection/perfectness

23. contentment   24. pleasure   25. anger

2-4 小練習

可數：1. 3. 4. 6. 7. 9. 13. 14. 15. 19. 21. 23. 24. 25.　　不可數：2. 5. 8. 10. 11. 12. 16. 17. 18. 20. 22. 26. 27. 28.

2-5 小練習（本大題無標準答案，以下所列僅供參考）

1. panel　　2. blocks　　3. flight　　4. army　　5. gust　　6. group; pool　　7. litter　　8. chain; board

9. group/chain　　10. audience; troupe

應用練習

PART 1

1. the frames of the glasses　　2. Mary's desk　　3. Charles' dog　　4. crocodiles' skins

5. the pages of the book　　6. hens' cackling　　7. for goodness' sake　　8. the dog's barking

9. the sun's rays　　10. the petals of the flower　　11. the nibs of the pens　　12. the kitten's meow

13. the colors of the paintings　　14. teachers' meeting　　15. old wives' tales　　16. children's mother

17. an hour's ride　　18. James' notebooks

PART 2

1. the lioness' cubs　　2. the cover of the pen　　3. the flowers of the plant　　4. Richard's watch

5. the flies' hairy legs　　6. no one else's place　　7. fifty cents' worth　　8. the moon's orbit

9. the tigress' roar　　10. the sheaves of corn　　11. the coaches of the train　　12. Japan's economy

13. yesterday's accident　　14. the village fool's antics　　15. four months' vacation

16. Great Britain's trade　　17. the tops of the bottles　　18. China's population　　19. an hour's delay

20. for vanity's sake　　21. the Coopers' house　　22. Napoleon the Third's reign

PART 3

1. two hours' wait　　2. the insects' wings　　3. the color of the pencil　　4. Russia's policy

5. at my wits' end　　6. the roots of the tree　　7. the lid of the box　　8. a year's work

9. the students of the school　　10. the roof of the house　　11. the girl's handbag

12. the animals of the jungle　　13. the doors of the car　　14. out of harm's way　　15. the lion's mane

16. Hong Kong's land problem　　17. Pluto's diameter　　18. the creatures of the sea

19. the force of the wind　　20. the bridesmaids' bouquets　　21. the cover of the flask

22. the formation of the volcano　　23. the Chief of Police's program　　24. in my mind's eye

PART 4

1. George's mistake　　2. Mr. Potter's papers　　3. the prince's horse　　4. teachers' union

5. my parents' idea　　6. someone else's money　　7. the dog's collar　　8. two hours' study

9. a week's holiday　　10. the actress' jewels　　11. the monkey's chatter　　12. Mr. James' suggestion

13. ten minutes' wait　　14. the shopkeeper's goods　　15. the teacher-in-charge's help

16. the chief officer's pay　　17. my sister-in-law's furniture　　18. the waitresses' attitude

PART 5

1. headmaster's   2. New Year's Eve; Helen's   3. man's; man's   4. Sally's   5. ladies'

6. sun's; Agnes'   7. week's; Charles'   8. children's; Billy's   9. goodness'; hour's

10. Miss Brown's; St. Philip Girls' School   11. Elsie's; Jeffrey's   12. Mrs. Smith's; ant's

13. James'   14. gentlemen's   15. Lois'; Mary's

PART 6

1. brother's/brothers'; wasp's; gardener's   2. mother's; dog's; days'   3. Heaven's; Thomas'

4. chicken's; chicken's   5. brother's; brothers'   6. butcher's; A's; parents'

7. teacher's; h's; l's; s's; z's   8. Mary's; parents-in-law's; husband's   9. Man's; astronauts'; moon's

10. bridesmaids'; bride's; bride's   11. brother's; someone else's; Stephen's   12. uncle's; fortnight's

13. dogs'; baby's; baby's   14. R's; p's; q's   15. weeks'; grandfather's; day's   16. witnesses'; snail's

PART 7

1. person's   2. brother's; else's   3. month's; sister's   4. witness'; client's   5. sun's; earth's

6. warriors'   7. mechanic's   8. owl's; child's   9. Betty's; parents'   10. Tom's; slave's

11. sun's; moment's   12. sister's; friend's; stone's; other's   13. boys'   14. days'; grandparents'

15. man's; dollars'

PART 8

1. cargoes   2. geese   3. foxes   4. roofs   5. boots   6. fishermen   7. passengers   8. pianos

9. mosquito(e)s   10. mice   11. houses   12. lice   13. bureaux/bureaus   14. fungi   15. sisters-in-law

16. grandmothers   17. passers-by   18. larvae   19. salmon   20. armfuls

PART 9

1. axes   2. ✕   3. families   4. curries   5. ✕   6. ✕   7. choruses   8. sciences   9. cacti

10. crises   11. media   12. geniuses/genii   13. indexes/indices   14. Mondays   15. echoes

PART 10

1. The children are crying for their mothers.   2. There are mice in the kitchen.   3. Those trucks are carrying cement to the factories.   4. They know the names of the clerks working in the office.   5. Lives were lost in the fire last night.   6. Flies are settling on the food that you have placed on the table. 7. There are easy ways to do these sums.   8. The LED lights on their bicycles are not working.   9. There are farms at the foot of the mountains.   10. Mosquito(e)s are insects.   11. The flutes are made of bamboo, but the pianos are not.   12. Those volcano(e)s are active ones.   13. The armies retreated, leaving the bodies of their heroes behind.

PART 11

1. The thieves who snatched the ladies' handbags were caught.   2. The women were shocked, weren't they?   3. The larvae of the mosquito(e)s come up to the surface of the water to breathe.   4. Are there any remedies for these types of sicknesses?   5. Our sisters-in-law like fish.   6. The farmers were carrying armfuls of hay into the barns.   7. The foremen ordered the workers to report to the managers.   8. The doorbells of those houses have been out of order since last week, haven't they?   9. We measured the radii of the circles and wrote the figures down in our notebooks.   10. These phenomena can be explained, can't they?   11. The cowherds were driving the cattle home when they were attacked by bandits.   12. The pupae/pupas change into butterflies after a few weeks, don't they?   13. The children's acts amused the audience a great deal.   14. The headmen were very proud of their sons-in-law.   15. We discovered that the can openers were rusty and that the rust had got into the cans of milk.

PART 12

1. The passers-by stopped and stared at the crying children.   2. The artists have studios in the apartments, don't they?   3. Do your cars always have breakdowns in the middle of the roads?   4. Lice are small insects living on the bodies of animals.   5. The cooks were measuring cupfuls of sugar into the mixing bowls.   6. On Fridays the gentlemen like to take walks along the cliffs.   7. The washerwomen were hanging up the shirts on the clothes-lines.   8. The roofs of the mud houses have gutter pipes to lead the water away when it rains.   9. Are the officers-in-charge supposed to collect the reports from the cadets?   10. There were traffic games in the playgrounds for the children during Road Safety Weeks.   11. There are large rooms with French windows in the houses.   12. The maids set mousetraps to catch the mice, but they were clever enough to avoid them.

PART 13

1. work; works   2. glass; glasses   3. kindnesses; kindness   4. art; arts   5. anxieties; anxiety
6. people; peoples   7. cruelties; Cruelty   8. love; loves   9. jealousies; jealousy
10. misery; miseries

PART 14

1. purity/pureness   2. cleanness   3. judgment   4. efficiency   5. speech   6. cleverness
7. simplicity   8. accuracy   9. opposition   10. reduction   11. explanation   12. punctuality
13. marriage   14. vacancy   15. application   16. ugliness   17. belief   18. breath   19. criticism/critic
20. reliance   21. dependence   22. conductor/conduction   23. moisture   24. success

PART 15

1. allocation   2. omission   3. choice   4. analysis   5. prophecy   6. obedience   7. division

8. life   9. denial   10. death   11. personification   12. hatred   13. splendor   14. excess

15. shortage   16. receiver/reception

PART 16

1. Knowledge; practice   2. irregularity; attendance   3. imagination   4. Success; contempt

5. recovery; effectiveness   6. arrival; happiness   7. frustration; contents   8. recognition; deed

9. speech; necessity; examination   10. justice; equality   11. promotion; tourism; concern

12. intelligence; admission   13. belief; youth; beauty   14. loyalty; devotion   15. choice; agreement

16. death; grief; burial   17. wrapping; shipment   18. writing; assistance

PART 17

1. anger; treatment; prisoners   2. work; satisfaction; production; goods

3. belief; judgment; men; men   4. exception; teacher; appearance   5. pronunciation; emphasis

6. announcement; explanation; manager   7. safety; refugees; government; settlement

8. confession; murderer; revelation; suspicion   9. occupants; inspection; permission

10. conclusion; meeting; announcement; resignation   11. invasion; foreigners; confusion; inhabitants

12. defense; selection; strength; valiancy   13. creation; mystery; solution

14. simplicity; innocence; adulthood; reality   15. suggestion; reduction; workers

16. expression; movements; anxiety; loss

PART 18

1. destruction; majority; insurance; construction   2. addition; subtraction; multiplication; division

3. opposition; suggestions   4. exposure   5. inspiration; artists   7. reassurance

8. rivalry; competition   9. efficiency; promotion   10. weight   11. bravery   12. trial; punishment

13. cowardice   14. advice; references   15. offense

PART 19

1. many; any   2. much   3. many; a few   4. many   5. a little; much   6. much; any

7. a few; much   8. much; a few   9. much; a little   10. many; a few   11. any; a little

12. any; a few   13. many; a few   14. any; a few   15. many; a few

PART 20

1. has; his   2. were   3. has   4. is   5. has; are   6. think; has   7. is; has   8. were; they

9. has; are   10. have   11. are; is   12. have; are   13. were; wasn't   14. is; has   15. isn't; are; are; are

Part 21

1. many　　2. was; has　　3. Many; are　　4. have; was　　5. is; a little; some

6. was; much; were; those　　7. aren't; any; was　　8. A large amount; has; it　　9. isn't; much; have; is

10. was; much; was; little

Part 22

1. Many; are　　2. A large amount; is　　3. weren't; many; a few　　4. flock; was　　5. A little; is

6. team; was　　7. A great number; have　　8. Were; a lot　　9. isn't; much　　10. nest; was

11. A group; has　　12. wasn't; much　　13. troop; has; a great deal　　14. A bunch; costs; a few

15. A lot; has; are　　16. A great deal of; has　　17. Were; a lot of　　18. A large amount; was

Chapter 3　解答

3-1 小練習

1. it; it　　2. they; them　　3. they; them　　4. it; it　　5. they; them　　6. they; them　　7. it; it

8. we; us　　9. you; you　　10. she; her　　11. they; them　　12. they; them　　13. he; him

14. he/she; him/her　　15. they; them　　16. he/she; him/her　　17. they; them　　18. they; them　　19. he; him

20. it; it

3-2 小練習

1. his; yours　　2. Hers; yours　　3. mine; hers　　4. ours; yours　　5. theirs; ours　　6. hers; mine

7. theirs　　8. hers; mine　　9. Ours; theirs　　10. mine; yours　　11. His; hers　　12. theirs; ours

13. His; yours; hers　　14. His; mine　　15. his; yours　　16. ours; yours　　17. ours　　18. theirs; his

3-3 小練習

1. himself　　2. myself　　3. themselves　　4. himself　　5. ourselves; himself/herself

6. himself/herself　　7. themselves　　8. herself　　9. myself; yourselves　　10. itself; themselves

11. himself; themselves; himself　　12. yourselves　　13. yourself; herself　　14. itself; himself

15. ourselves; themselves　　16. herself; herself　　17. herself; themselves　　18. yourself; himself

19. themselves; ourselves

應用練習

PART 1

1. He; her; she　　2. She; him; me; you　　3. they; her　　4. him; He　　5. them; they　　6. He; us

7. us　　8. her; she　　9. me; he　　10. us; him　　11. me; He; us　　12. they　　13. I　　14. him; me

15. It　　16. they; we　　17. they　　18. her; I; her; I　　19. him; they　　20. her; him; they

PART 2

1. us; They   2. her; her; him   3. them; us; they; we/us   4. we; them; they; us

5. her; her; her; her   6. she; her   7. him; she; me   8. I; her; she; it   9. she; him; she; he/him

10. me; they; They; I   11. me; him; them; us; him   12. he; I; her   13. it; it   14. He; he

15. She/It; she/it; her/it; she/it   16. us; we; her   17. he; they; he   18. I; I; it; it; they; I; them; me

PART 3

1. him; He   2. me   3. they   4. We; them   5. me   6. me; her   7. him   8. him; they

9. We; It; us; it 10. They; we/us; We; we; they/them   11. she; me; it; her   12. she; us

13. they; he; him; they   14. he/him; she; he/him   15. him; he; it; him

PART 4

1. He told us about it.   2. They sent the driver to fetch her from school.   3. They spent it at the racetrack.   4. We put them into it.   5. He caught it in the garden yesterday.   6. She does not allow him to stay up late.   7. They have got off it.   8. She showed it to them   9. It skidded when he was driving on the highway.   10. We saw him in town, but he did not recognize us.   11. Was she late for it yesterday?   12. Please tell him not to seek shelter under them during a storm.   13. The water she drank from it has made her very ill.   14. You can wear them if you like.   15. We have written them in it.   16. It is dirty. You cannot sleep in it until she has cleaned it.

PART 5

1. We decided to visit her this weekend.   2. He told him not to make it again.   3. Don't tell them that we have forgotten to bring it.   4. They are not going to buy it. They say that it is too expensive.   5. He bought them from her.   6. She said that we should never do it again.   7. Have they gone home yet? They were just telling her that they were tired.   8. They had bought it as a birthday present for him.   9. He was walking down the road when he bumped into it.   10. It was trying to catch them when it knocked the bottle of milk over.   11. Many of them think that they have lost their chance for it.   12. We told them that they must find another place to do it.   13. They say that she is not coming to the meeting because she is not feeling well.   14. You are going to get into trouble if you persist in calling them freaks.   15. We did not enjoy it at all. Did you like it?

PART 6

1. They have gone to see it.   2. She parked it near the telephone booth and went to look for them.   3. He/She told the players about them.   4. She lost the key to it, so they had to wait till he returned home.   5. It is used by them. I wonder if they find it useful.   6. It reached us when we were playing basketball.

7. They called out to him when they recognized him as their uncle.   8. They wanted to buy the same dress. It was the only one left in the shop. She tried to find something else for one of the women.   9. We saw the ships when they sailed into the harbor.   10. They asked her about him.   11. My brother asked him for it, so he gave it to him.   12. They hid them in it. They did not know that it would be flooded during high tide.   13. They will be published in the local newspaper. We are waiting anxiously for them.   14. It reached them when they were in the midst of their examination.   15. They looked so delicious that she could not resist buying some of them.   16. He found it while he was digging in the garden yesterday.   17. He is going to drive us to the airport tomorrow. We don't need to depend on Mr. Smith for transport.   18. They did not prevent my uncle from exploring farther up the river as he had a very competent guide with him.   19. They have told her the truth, but she does not believe them at all.   20. She came over to our table as soon as we had sat down. She handed a menu to us and waited to take down our order.

PART 7

1. He imitated it.   2. He sent him to look for us.   3. Do they eat nuts?   4. We are going to the trade fair this afternoon.   5. She bought them from him/her.   6. He dug them up with it.   7. Would you tell her about them?   8. It is making them shiver.   9. He would not accept any of them.   10. He repaired it for her.   11. They were good friends in their school days.   12. Don't tell us that you lost your way.   13. We can't find it anywhere. Have you hidden it?   14. They are flying around the lights again. Please ask him to do something about them.   15. They brought it for her.   16. He lost the key to it.   17. They were dying, so I told him/her to put them in the shade.   18. Was he waiting for it yesterday?

PART 8

1. His look newer than mine though we bought ours at the same time. I wonder how he kept his in such good condition.   2. I know this is either yours or his. It's too big to be hers.   3. I am sharpening mine. Do you want me to sharpen yours? You may as well as bring his, too. I can sharpen yours together.   4. Theirs have got mixed up with ours. They should not have put theirs here. This shelf is ours; theirs is just beside ours.   5. Mine is broken. I can't use hers because it is broken, too. May I borrow yours?   6. We have finished ours. They haven't even started on theirs. I don't think that they will finish theirs in time. What about yours?   7. They must be friends of his. The car they're driving is his.   8. I can't find mine anywhere. This one is his and that is hers. Yours is here, too. Where can mine be?   9. That dog is not ours; it is theirs. It has eaten our dog's dinner.   10. Those friends of his think that theirs is the

only car on the road. They drove theirs in the center of the road and did not allow ours to pass.   11. He has taken his, not yours. Let's go riding together. You take yours and I'll take mine.   12. Our teacher has corrected ours, but not theirs. She said that they did theirs in such a slipshod manner that she refused to correct them.   13. Can I borrow a racket of hers? Which of these are hers? I broke mine when I was playing with Allen. He did not break his.   14. The car is his. Sometimes he gives me permission to use his, unlike my sister who always refuses to let me drive hers.   15. Have you seen mine? I've searched everywhere but I can see only yours and hers. I wondered if a friend of hers has taken mine by mistake.   16. She forgot to bring hers and asked me to lend her mine. But as mine was broken, she borrowed his.   17. We have bought ours for tonight's performance but we did not buy his and hers. They can buy theirs tonight.   18. Theirs is fierce but ours is fiercer. Ours not only barks at strangers but bites them, too. As for theirs, its bark is worse than its bite. Yours is fiercer than theirs, too.   19. This bag is mine and that is yours. I know that hers has a buckle which distinguishes it from their and ours.

PART 9

1. Did you see mine anywhere?   2. They seem to have lost theirs, too.   3. Hers has white lace on it. What is yours like?   4. No, I don't think that is mine. It must be hers.   5. Do you think you will need ours as well as theirs?   6. I think that this is his, not yours.   7. He borrowed mine because he had lost his.   8. All his have been given away to the village children.   9. He is wearing his. Why aren't you wearing yours?   10. "Are these yours?" "No, they are not mine. They must be theirs!"   11. We must divide this equally. This will be yours, and that will be ours.   12. I was just finishing mine when she started to do hers.   13. Hers look the same as mine, but mine are more expensive than hers.   14. I hope that they have not taken ours together with theirs. My mother told me to bring ours back today.   15. Most of the girls have brought theirs with them. Did you bring yours, too? I brought mine, but Andy didn't bring his. He asked me to share mine with him.

PART 10

1. He has forgotten to bring his, so I am sharing mine with him.   2. Mine is nearby, but hers is further away.   3. Your writing is not as neat as hers, but I still prefer yours.   4. "Which of these sweets are theirs and which are ours?" he asked.   5. After Mr. Smith has marked hers, he will mark ours.   6. "Let me have a look at yours and I'll show you mine," I told him.   7. That house with the red roof is hers and mine is just next door.   8. I couldn't find mine, but I saw his under the bed, and yours were just behind the cupboard.   9. She says that the bracelet is hers, but I am quite sure it is mine.   10. I think this bag is his, not hers, because I have often seen him using it.   11. As soon as we have done ours,

we will help you finish yours.　12. They gave me one of theirs, but I couldn't give them mine as I didn't have one with me then.　13. When Lucy finished hers, she took some of his.　14. Eddie's shirt is being dried at the moment, so he has to wear one of mine.　15. He said he could lend us one of his, but we brought ours just the same.　16. Yours and his look the same except for the difference in color.　17. I cheeked hers while she checked mine.　18. We had looked into all the drawers—hers, mine, and even his, but it wasn't in any of them.

PART 11

1. This is mine, and that is yours.　2. He had finished eating his before I had started on mine.　3. They were unwrapping theirs while we were unwrapping ours.　4. She is wearing hers. Where are yours?　5. That knife is his, but those bags are hers.　6. Theirs have names on them.　7. Are these yours or mine?　8. I think this is theirs and that is his.　9. We have been to his, but we haven't been to hers.　10. Do you need ours as well as hers?　11. That cat is hers. It is not theirs.　12. Are these ours? We do not want to use theirs.　13. Hers look newer than mine though both of us bought ours at the same time.

PART 12

1. themselves; himself　2. himself; ourselves　3. yourself; themselves

4. myself; himself; yourself　5. themselves; himself　6. himself; myself; herself

7. himself; itself; himself　8. themselves; himself　9. themselves; herself　10. themselves; itself

11. yourself; himself; themselves　12. himself; themselves　13. ourselves; himself; myself

14. myself; yourself; yourself　15. herself; himself/herself; themselves　16. himself; himself; herself

17. himself

PART 13

1. ourselves　2. themselves　3. yourselves　4. himself　5. themselves　6. myself; himself

7. ourselves; themselves　8. myself; themselves　9. ourselves; himself　10. myself; myself

11. yourself; myself　12. itself; himself　13. yourself/yourselves; themselves　14. ourselves; himself

PART 14

1. himself　2. himself　3. ourselves　4. himself　5. himself/herself　6. yourself　7. herself

8. himself　9. herself　10. ourselves; herself　11. yourselves　12. themselves　13. himself

14. itself　15. itself　16. themselves　17. myself; himself　18. himself; itself　19. themselves; itself

20. yourselves; myself

PART 15

1. himself   2. himself; herself   3. themselves; yourself/yourselves   4. myself; yourselves

5. himself/herself   6. yourselves; herself   7. ourselves   8. itself   9. himself   10. ourselves

11. themselves   12. herself; myself   13. themselves   14. themselves; himself   15. ourselves; himself

PART 16

1. herself   2. his; mine; himself   3. itself   4. ourselves; yours   5. himself; his; himself

6. myself; hers   7. hers   8. itself   9. Theirs; myself   10. hers; his; ourselves   11. herself; hers

12. yourselves; himself   13. themselves; theirs   14. herself; hers; ourselves

Chapter 4　解答

4–1 小練習

1. who   2. whom   3. whom   4. who   5. whom   6. who   7. who   8. whom   9. who

10. whom   11. whom   12. whom

4–3 小練習

1. that   2. which; that   3. whom   4. who   5. who   6. whom   7. which   8. whom

9. whose   10. who   11. who   12. who   13. who   14. whose   15. whose   16. which

17. who   18. which   19. which   20. which

4–4 小練習

1. The mistake he made is very serious.   2. The handbag she lost contains a lot of money.   3. The person I am writing to is a total stranger.   4. The girl I took this from has disappeared.   5. The cake my sister baked this morning is very delicious.   6. The watch she is wearing is a brand-new one.   7. The lady you helped yesterday is my mother.   8. The boy I entrusted the bag to has brought it back.   9. The songs he composed will be sung at the concert.   10. She has bought all the things she needs for the party.   11. The bench he is sitting on is still wet with paint.   12. The album they are looking at is my brother's.   13. Has the knife you sharpened just now been put in a safe place?

4–5 小練習

1. whose   2. which   3. whom   4. whose   5. which   6. who   7. whom   8. whose

9. which   10. which   11. whom   12. whom   13. whom   14. which   15. whom   16. who

17. whose   18. which   19. whom   20. which

4–6 小練習

1. He bought a big bunch of grapes, half of which were sour.   2. She found the box, the cover of which was dented.   3. I have thrown away the book, the pages of which were torn.   4. I examined those

antiques, a few of which were priceless.　5. She has sent the shoes, the heels of which were worn-out, to the cobbler.　6. A large crowd watched the play, most of which was hard to understand.　7. We enjoyed eating the food, all of which was delicious.　8. The cat gave birth to three kittens, two of which were white and brown.　9. He sent the watch, the spring of which was broken, to the repair shop.　10. This is the dress, the hem of which had been let down.　11. The box, the bottom of which had dropped out, has been thrown away.　12. The book, the cover of which is very attractive, is not interesting at all.　13. A wallet, the inside of which contained a photograph and some money, has been found.　14. Mother had baked a huge birthday cake, half of which was covered with cherries.　15. She had bought a kilogram of grapes, three quarters of which were rotten.　16. The carpenter has repaired the table, a leg of which was broken.　17. The players, three of whom were veterans, were victorious in the match.　18. These children, a few of whom are less than six years old, will take part in the play.

應用練習

PART 1

1. I have just written a thank you note to Mr. Taylor whose house I stayed in during the floods.　2. The person whom you bought the gold coins from is a swindler.　3. The scream came from the child whose teeth were being examined by the dentist.　4. Tell me about the little boy whose grandparents made him the heir to their fortune.　5. This is the man whom I gave your message to.　6. The manager is interviewing an applicant whom he thinks will be suitable for the job.　7. I spoke to a girl whose name is Alison about the activities of our club.　8. Will you please call the girl whose father has come to take her home?　9. The motorist whose license had not been renewed got into trouble with the traffic policeman.　10. The pilot of the helicopter whose arm was injured was forced to make a landing.　11. The architect whose design has been approved was congratulated.　12. The person whose life had been devoted to doing good deserves his popularity.

PART 2

1. Let me introduce you to the man whose paintings you admired so much.　2. The children whom we saw at the beach were enjoying themselves very much.　3. That is the nurse whom we were telling you about.　4. Here come the boys whom we have been waiting for.　5. You are the person whom everyone depends on.　6. I can't remember the fisherman whose boat we borrowed last summer.　7. He is a man whose temper flares up easily.　8. That is the team whom we have to play against in the finals.　9. Those are the workers whose salaries have been increased.　10. Show me a photograph of the girl whom you are corresponding with.　11. The boy whose friends gave him much support has been

elected chairman.   12. Where are the volunteers whom you are looking for?   13. The shout came from the lady whose house caught fire.   14. Some of the swimmers whom we were watching did some fancy dives.   15. I don't know the name of the boy whom I borrowed the dictionary from.   16. A reporter was taking photographs of the girl whose car was involved in the accident.   17. Can you take me to the person whom the order was issued by?   18. The man whose toes I accidentally stepped on glared at me.   19. He won't tell me the name of the man whom he got the news through.

PART 3

1. who   2. whom   3. whom   4. whom   5. who   6. who   7. whom   8. who   9. who
10. who   11. whom   12. whom

PART 4

1. whose   2. whom   3. which; which   4. which; who   5. who   6. who   7. who   8. whose
9. whom   10. that   11. whose   12. whom   13. whom   14. whom   15. who   16. who   17. whom
18. who

PART 5

1. The camera which he gave (to) me for my birthday is made in Germany.   2. Tell her about the snake which we killed yesterday.   3. The boys who took the apples live next door.   4. The person who beats me at chess will get this album.   5. The performance which we saw today was very good.   6. The postman who usually brings our letters is on leave.   7. He took the pills which were strong enough to make him fall into a deep sleep.   8. The army captain who died in an accident on Saturday was a very brave man.   9. Where is the pair of scissors which she lent (to) you yesterday?   10. We congratulated the student who won a prize for good conduct.   11. Mr. West is very proud of his antique telephone which he bought at an auction.   12. The salesman who sold you the vacuum cleaner is from our firm.   13. That is the best film that I have ever seen.   14. Did you read in the newspapers about the boy who helped the soldiers find a missing helicopter in the jungle?   15. They are bringing some cakes which are very delicious.

PART 6

1. They found some golf balls which he lost yesterday.   2. We spoke to the lady who sold the magazines to us.   3. I have a friend whose brother works in the Customs Office.   4. We went to a wedding which took place at the bride's house.   5. Let me introduce you to the woman whose daughter won first prize in the cooking contest.   6. Peter is the boy whom we all voted for.   7. The man who came to our house just now is a plumber.   8. The guests whom we invited this morning did not come.

9. The bird which you saw on the steps just now is a wood pigeon.   10. I told him about the storm which destroyed several houses last week.   11. He kept a record of his employees who were often late for work.   12. The man whom we gave a glass of water to was sick.   13. My friend whom I lent the scooter to last night has not returned it yet.   14. The girl whose handiwork you saw just now is blind and deaf.   15. They broke the promise which they made before they left.

PART 7

1. This is the book which they quarreled over.   2. He unwrapped the present which I had given him.   3. That is the chair which he was sitting on.   4. There is a limit which nobody can go beyond.   5. He will take you to the laboratory which they have spent a million dollars on.   6. The party which obtains the most votes will form the next government.   7. I think this is the route which the hikers took.   8. Have you found the key which everybody is looking for?   9. Mary explained the procedure which I was to follow to me.   10. I am certain this is the diary which he writes down his appointments in.   11. The team which scores the most points will be declared the winner.   12. He tried to brush off the ants which were crawling all over his body.   13. This is the tunnel which the train travels through.   14. She hung the clothes which she had washed earlier in the garden.   15. This is the room which he keeps all his camera equipment in.

PART 8

1. whose   2. whom; who   3. whose   4. whom   5. whose   6. whom   7. which   8. which
9. whose   10. which   11. who   12. who   13. whom   14. who   15. whom   16. who   17. whom
18. who; whom

PART 9

1. The postman, whose leg was bitten by a mad dog, has been sent to the hospital.   2. Irene, whom most people think is a shy girl, recited a poem at the concert.   3. Lauren, whom I walked home with last night, lives nearby.   4. The girl, whom you borrowed the umbrella from yesterday, wants it back now.   5. Mr. Smith, whose horse just won the race, is a well-known horse trainer.   6. The man, whom you saw standing beside me yesterday, is my father.   7. The artist, whose paintings you admired at the exhibition, has gone abroad.   8. Mr. Gray, whom I introduced you to last night, is working in this bank.   9. My uncle, who lives near the sea on the East Coast, possesses a wonderful collection of coral.
10. Benny, who lived next door to me, has gone to the university to study law.   11. Elephants, which are valued for their tusks, are hunted by an increasing number of people.   12. Paul, whose cousin is your neighbor, has gone to America.   13. Betty, whom you were introduced to at Paul's house, would like to

invite you to her party.　14. Mr. Robinson, whom I have great respect for, will be coming here soon. 15. My brother, whom I gave your message to, seems very pleased with you.　16. Maria, whose English is of a very high standard, has been chosen as the winner of the essay competition.　17. The boys, whose football match is on Saturday, have decided not to go on the picnic.　18. Your friend, whom you are going with to Happy Valley , has arrived with all his luggage.

PART 10

1. Mr. Paul Jones, whose brother is our neighbor, is going to Canada next month.　2. Mrs. Smith, who twisted her ankle yesterday, has to walk on crutches for a few days.　3. The man, whom I saw you talking to this morning, is waiting outside for you.　4. Mr. Mason, whose son won the prize for being the best student in his class, is very pleased and happy.　5. My brother, who is studying in the United Kingdom , will come home next week.　6. This supermarket belongs to Mr. Harrison, who is a very rich man.　7. Jeanette, who went to Europe a year ago, has just come back.　8. That girl, whose brother is a friend of my brother's, always comes to my house.　9. Justin Reynolds, whose ambition and personality made him the top man in the firm, is much admired.　10. Her younger brother, who was with her, saw the accident, too.　11. That team, which had broken the rules, was expelled from the tournament.　12. He washed the glasses, which was all he would do for us.　13. They changed all the locks in the house, which was a very wise thing to do.　14. Mosquitoes, which can be found in swampy areas, breed very fast.　15. His friend, whose brother was a doctor, accompanied him to the hospital. 16. The man in front of me, whose name I do not know, was talking very loudly.　17. Beethoven, whose music is among the finest in the world, became deaf during his later years.　18. Mr. Cooper, whose work confines him to the office, goes hunting whenever he can.　19. Madame Curie, whose name is down in history as one of the greatest women of our age, discovered radium.

PART 11

1. I invited a few friends, one of whom was my former classmate.　2. He told me that only twenty persons, the majority of whom were boys, passed the test.　3. We brought along some sandwiches, most of which were eaten by Jim.　4. They discovered an important letter, parts of which were burned and charred.　5. Fifteen people, some of whom were suspected to be children, were believed to have been killed.　6. They sent him many letters, only two of which he replied to.　7. There were some guests, one of whom was an Australian, staying at his house.　8. Eight people, three of whom were members of the crew, survived the crash.　9. There were some faint letters, two of which were distinguishable, carved on the monument.　10. In the desk was an old book, the cover of which was torn.

11. He showed her some ladies' hats, none of which was to her liking.　12. Mrs. Ford bought a scarf, the border of which was made of lace.　13. More than sixty thousand people, many of whom were from abroad, came to watch the match.　14. We wrote to about thirty people, most of whom never bothered to reply.　15. Paul took part in many contests, a few of which were at an international level.　16. Four others guys, one of whom was a professor, joined in at the last moment.　17. There were only three Asians on the ship, two of whom were tourists.　18. The bellboy brought in a large suitcase, the top of which was stamped with the names of various countries.　19. He gained a lot of profit, half of which was given to his partner.

PART 12

1. who　2. which　3. whose　4. whom　5. whom　6. which　7. that　8. that　9. whom
10. that

PART 13

1. She scolded the man who stepped on her foot.　2. I saw the carpet which you wanted to buy.　3. We met the salesman who came to our house yesterday.　4. These are the men who rescued the children from the burning house.　5. Can you show me the road which leads to the railway station?　6. The goat which was tied to the tree has been stolen.　7. She burned the letter which she received this morning.　8. The boys who are in the other room need to be taught a lesson.　9. I'll invite my friends who live opposite us.　10. He threw away the shirt which was torn.　11. He killed the caterpillars which he found on the leaves of his tree.　12. My brother who fell from a ladder is to be discharged from the hospital soon.　13. There are several potholes in the road which badly need repairing.　14. The guests who arrived at the hotel this morning have gone sightseeing.　15. They are the best football team that ever played for our school.　16. The men who work at the garage here have gone home for lunch.

PART 14

1. Is that the boy who saved the child from drowning?　2. He asked me about the bicycle which he had left outside the shed.　3. She showed us the embroidery piece which she had been working on the whole week.　4. Do you know the contestant who is wearing a red sweater?　5. I closed the window which was banging about in the wind.　6. That car belongs to the man who lives in that big house.　7. We want to get tickets for the show which starts at seven o'clock.　8. There is something that I must tell you about.　9. The snake which bit the man was identified as a viper.　10. My brother pointed excitedly at the man who had just boarded the bus.　11. Should I tell you about the stranger who knocked at my door late one night?　12. He pointed to the house which was standing forlornly on the

hilltop.　13. The flats which were partly destroyed in the fire are to be pulled down.　14. The tie which he bought in Hawaii looks nice on him.　15. I saw two men who were lurking suspiciously near the bushes.　16. This is one of the things which money cannot buy.　17. That is the boy who kicked the ball through our window.

PART 15

1. That is the hotel which my friend told me about.　2. The boy who lives next door is a big bully. 3. She threw away all the vegetables which were turning bad.　4. That is the boy who saved me from drowning in that pool.　5. He showed me the bicycle which his father had given to him for his birthday. 6. My mother threw away the box which contained all my comics and storybooks.　7. This is the first time that I have played volleyball.　8. My parents have gone to see the house which had been put up for rent.　9. Mary had a little lamb which followed her to school every day.　10. Many of the children went hunting for the treasure which Miss Brown had hidden somewhere.　11. The man who is responsible for this crime must be brought to justice.　12. She scolded the child for throwing stones at the dog which belonged to the neighbors.　13. The boy who stole the silver cup is going to be punished by the teacher.　14. The dog which had bitten the little girl who lives down the street has been shot.

PART 16

1. Those are the people whose homes were destroyed in the flood.　2. You must meet Dr. Peters, whom I have already told you about.　3. Mary told us about her neighbor whose son had been killed in an accident.　4. Many students whose fathers are too poor to send them to school are given free books and education.　5. They said that they were going to visit the old lady whose daughter had just run away.　6. Where is the girl whom you were talking to a few minutes ago?　7. The man whose daughter is in your class is waiting outside in his car.　8. Those children whose parents have arrived can go now.　9. The girl whom I borrowed the umbrella from is talking to her friends in the garden.

PART 17

1. They went to see the old lady whose son is a famous lawyer.　2. He was riding on his new bicycle which his uncle had given to him for his birthday.　3. She grew fond of the cat which she had found on the way to school.　4. The girl whom I was talking to a few minutes ago has to go home as soon as possible.　5. Mrs. Black scolded the little boy who had pulled her cat's tail.　6. The books which are on the table over there should be returned to the school library tomorrow.　7. All the children who like to watch Mickey Mouse want to see this film.　8. There are many people in the world today who live only for pleasure and amusement.　9. The bird which you can see in its cage near the door is called a

'cockatoo.'   10. The girl whom I passed on the road just now was wearing a beautiful, red dress with matching shoes and handbag.   11. The suitcase which I like very much is too expensive for me.   12. The girl whose bag had been stolen has been advised to make a report at the police station.   13. I would like all of you to meet my cousin Belinda, who has come to my house for a short visit.

PART 18

1. I heard a story which frightened me very much.   2. The girl whom my sister is sharing a room with is very friendly.   3. The spectators who were watching the football match cheered loudly.   4. The cat which belongs to my youngest niece sleeps in that basket.   5. Do you see the boy whom we were talking about yesterday?   6. That girl whose sister is a fashion designer works in my office.   7. Did I tell you about the stranger whom I met as I was walking home?   8. The lady who is wearing the green dress is my aunt.   9. My brother brought home a basket of eggs, half of which were rotten.   10. The boys, five of whom were scouts, spent their holidays camping in Lighthouse Island.   11. He wrote to his friend who was studying in London.   12. That boy whom Lucy is talking to now is my brother.   13. The cat which is sleeping under the table is a Siamese cat.   14. The meeting which was fixed for today may be postponed.   15. Our school team, two members of which are my classmates, won the match.   16. My younger brother bought some goldfish which he kept in a tank.   17. Everyone mourned the death of that man, whose acts of charity and generosity had made him popular.   18. Aunt Mary sent the orphanage a box of old toys, most of which were still in a very good condition.   19. Henry wants to return the books which he borrowed from you last month.   20. The kittens whose mother was dead cried pathetically.

Chapter 5 解答

5-1 小練習

1. either; or   2. either; or   3. Either; or   4. neither; nor   5. neither; nor   6. Neither; nor
7. and   8. but   9. and   10. and   11. but   12. and   13. but   14. and   15. and; but   16. and; and
17. or   18. so/and   19. or   20. or   21. or   22. either; or   23. Neither; nor   24. Neither; nor
25. either; or; neither; nor   26. or   27. Neither; nor

5-2 小練習

1. wherever   2. unless; as   3. as; as   4. where; even; though   5. as/so; as; though/although
6. since; than   7. as; if/though; though/although   8. When; as; as; where   9. as/so; as; than
10. If/When/Whenever; even; though/if   11. before; unless   12. Although/Though; whenever

13. as; even; if   14. while; if; as; if/though   15. Even; though; whenever   16. where; though/although

應用練習

PART 1

1. if   2. as; as   3. so/as; as   4. when/as/while   5. because/as   6. as; if/though

7. as; if/though   8. While/When/As   9. whenever; if   10. as/so; as; though/although

11. Even; though   12. as; as; if   13. as/because; However   14. Although/Though; so/as; as   15. If

PART 2

1. since/because/as   2. although/though   3. as/because/since   4. so; that   5. and   6. so

7. as/because/since   8. Even; though   9. but/yet   10. either; or   11. because/as/since   12. nor

13. but/yet   14. Although/Though; as/because/since   15. but/yet   16. Although/Though

PART 3

1. and   2. Even; though   3. and   4. and   5. and; but/yet   6. but/yet   7. and   8. but/yet

9. Though/Although; and   10. and; but/yet   11. and; although/though   12. and

13. Although/Though   14. and; but/yet; though/although   15. Although/Though   16. or; else

17. such; that

PART 4

1. because/since/as   2. or   3. Either; or   4. and; but/yet   5. either; or   6. but/yet

7. Neither; nor   8. nor   9. and; because/since/as   10. but/yet; though/although   11. or; but/yet

12. although/though; and   13. and; but/yet   14. nor; because/as/since   15. nor   16. Although/Though

PART 5

1. because/since/as   2. although/though   3. either; or; but/yet   4. and; even; though

5. because/since/as   6. and   7. Although/Though   8. Neither; nor; because/since/as

9. or; but/yet   10. but/yet   11. because/since/as; and   12. and; because/since/as   13. because/since/as

14. either; or   15. because/since/as; and

PART 6

1. while/when/as   2. so   3. When/As/after   4. As/Since/Because   5. so; that   6. Even; though

7. and   8. either; or   9. Although/Though; and   10. neither; nor   11. When

12. As/When/While; so   13. so   14. When/As; Even; though; and   15. because/since/as; and; but/yet

16. so; that

PART 7

1. but/yet   2. and   3. but/yet   4. Although/Though   5. Even; though   6. but/yet

7. even; though   8. and   9. though/although   10. and   11. but/yet   12. even; though   13. and

14. but/yet   15. and; but/yet   16. Even; though; and   17. and; but/yet   18. and; but/yet; and

PART 8

1. even; though; so   2. nor; while/as/when   3. as; well; as; so   4. but/yet   5. moreover

6. or; so; that   7. When/As; and   8. and; but/yet; Therefore   9. yet/but   10. because/since/as; and

11. thus   12. Either; or; so; that   13. still   14. When; even; though   15. Since/Because/As

16. Although/Though; but; because/since/as   17. because/since/as; Also   18. so; so; that

19. nevertheless

PART 9

1. and; yet/but   2. not; only; but; also; so; that   3. Since/As/Because; so; that

4. as/since/because; Hence   5. or; else   6. as; well; as;   7. either; or; However; as/since/because

8. Although/Though; and; and   9. Both; and; as/because/since; but/yet   10. nevertheless/however/still

11. in; order; that; Nevertheless   12. but/yet; however; as/because/since

13. and; and; as/because/since; but   14. and; either; or   15. and; but/yet; and

PART 10（本大題無標準答案，以下所列僅供參考）

1. While we were watching television, all the lights went off.   2. I was afraid, but I did not show it.
3. They started early so that they could reach the station on time.   4. Although it was not very dark, he switched on the light.   5. They are blind, but they can do a lot of things.   6. Though we waited for another half hour, he did not appear.   7. Even though there was a slight drizzle, many people came to watch the game.   8. I tied up the boat in order that it wouldn't drift away.   9. As his mother was in the kitchen, he slipped in unnoticed.   10. Although they refused to tell me, I could guess what was going on.   11. Even though the jungle was dense with undergrowth, we managed to cut our way through.   12. While she was stepping off the bus, it started to move.   13. She searched all over the house, but she couldn't find the letter.   14. I left a light on, so the house wouldn't be in complete darkness.   15. When the club members were leaving the room, the chairman called out to them.   16. Though I warned Alex not to interfere in their business, he insists on doing so.   17. Although their school team had lost the match, they were not discouraged and they congratulated us.   18. It was dinner time, but Pauline was not hungry.   19. When I was on the bus, I saw Ben crossing the road, but he did not see me.   20. Although she wanted to leave without wasting time, she sat down to write a note to her uncle so that he wouldn't worry about her.

PART 11（本大題無標準答案，以下所列僅供參考）

1. I did not hear him come in because I was thinking about my work.　　2. There was so much noise that I could hardly hear him.　　3. They did the work as fast as possible so that they could go home in time for tea.　　4. My friends didn't come to my house because they were too busy with the arrangements.　　5. I wanted to go over to Sandra's house in order that I could meet Michael and James there.　　6. She was writing a letter to her pen pal when she suddenly heard a loud crash.　　7. She ran to the door quickly because she thought someone had fallen down the stairs.　　8. When I was watching her closely, I saw her take something from Peter's wallet.　　9. They put away their books and went out to play because it was already four o'clock.　　10. She copied down the poem so that she could read it to her younger sister.　　11. The room looked drab, so we cut some flowers and placed them in a vase on the table.　　12. She was very angry with me because she thought that I had pulled her hair in class.　　13. The old man tended the orchids carefully , for he wanted to win a prize in the Flower Show.　　14. As the servant was ironing some shirts, she heard a loud scream for help.

PART 12（本大題無標準答案，以下所列僅供參考）

1. Because she was ill, she did not go to the office but went to see a doctor.　　2. He ran fast because he wanted to catch the train.　　3. After she had washed the clothes, she hung them out to dry, but she took them back again when she saw dark clouds gathering in the sky.　　4. I have neither seen nor borrowed your book.　　5. He did not want to go home because he had done something very wrong.　　6. Even though the wind was strong and rain fell heavily, we managed to come.　　7. That boy did not complete his work because he was lazy, so the teacher punished him.　　8. You must hurry up, or you will be late for school.　　9. The river as well as the roads were flooded because it had been raining for many days.　　10. Pauline and Margaret ran fast, but Jane ran faster.　　11. The two men were weary and thirsty because they had walked under the hot desert sun for a long time.　　12. When the flood was over, people returned to their homes and found that everything had been destroyed.　　13. Neither Peter nor Thomas saw it, but there must be someone who had seen it.　　14. That girl speaks not only English but also many other foreign languages, so she is an outstanding student.　　15. We must do something quickly, or else she will fall into the river.　　16. I can never read as fast as she.

PART 13（本大題無標準答案，以下所列僅供參考）

1. He tried to stop the car when he saw the boy running across the road.　　2. I did not see your kitten, but I heard a kitten crying in my backyard.　　3. You must water those plants, or they will wither and die.　　4. He stepped out of his house, but he went in again because he saw dark clouds gathering in the sky.　　5. Robert and his brother can carve well.　　6. He likes to watch people swimming, but he has never

tried to swim before because he is afraid of water.　7. Although he is a wealthy man, he has very simple tastes and is generous to the needy, too.　8. I can run as fast as Linda, but I did not win a prize. 9. The cost of making a cement badminton court here can run up to two or three thousand dollars.　10. After he finished reading the letter, he felt very angry and burned it.　11. He lost his watch; so he dared not go home because his parents would scold him.　12. Mr. Jackson was very happy because he had won first prize in the lottery. Although he hadn't received his money yet, he gave his friends a big dinner. 13. After the fire had died down, they tried to salvage whatever they could find.　14. Even though the woman is very old, she is strong.

PART 14（本大題無標準答案，以下所列僅供參考）

1. He took careful aim with his pistol, but he missed the target.　2. The river burst its banks and flooded the whole town.　3. Ben did not switch on the fan even though he felt very hot.　4. The scouts soon had their tents set up and the fire lighted.　5. She cooked the vegetables and fried the fish, but she did not cook the meat.　6. He lighted his cigarette and threw the match on the floor.　7. There were two letters and three cards on the table.　8. The man was caught and sentenced to life imprisonment.　9. His family was poor, but he had never borrowed from anyone.　10. Though he tried very hard, he failed the examination.　11. Although they were hungry, they did not eat much at dinner. 12. Even though this man is deaf and dumb, he has a good job.　13. He fell from a tree and broke his left leg.

PART 15（本大題無標準答案，以下所列僅供參考）

1. Robin bought the checked shirt because he liked it.　2. It was raining hard, so they had to stay indoors.　3. The tunnel was dark and narrow.　4. Their car ran out of gas, so they had to walk to the nearest village to get some.　5. There was neither electricity nor proper water supply in the village. 6. Do you sleep in this room or in the other one?　7. The journey was slow because one of the scouts had twisted his ankle.　8. I have neither taken your book nor seen it anywhere.　9. She took a pair of scissors and cut the string in two.　10. The man refused to ferry us across because the river was too swift and dangerous.　11. The door was left slightly open, so I could hear every word they said.　12. The hawk swooped down and snatched the chicken away.　13. You can pass in your book either today or tomorrow.　14. All of us were tired and hungry.　15. He was tied securely, so he could neither move nor call out.　16. Mr. Mason broke a traffic law, so he had to pay a fine or be imprisoned for one month.

PART 16（本大題無標準答案，以下所列僅供參考）

1. He needs a haircut badly; however, the barber shop is closed today.　2. A fishbone was stuck in her

throat; therefore, she couldn't swallow her food.　　3. They were very tired after their long climb uphill; hence, they walked to the tree and sat down under it.　　4. He was very busy; nevertheless, he found time to write to his parents.　　5. She bought a box of soap powder from the salesman; still, he refused to leave and wanted her to buy something else.　　6. It was raining; however, we decided to go.　　7. Tony swam very well; nevertheless, he did not win the competition.　　8. You can choose either this puppy or that one; however, you cannot have both of them.

PART 17 （本大題無標準答案，以下所列僅供參考）

1. I used torchlight since it was very dark by then.　　2. I wanted to go with them very badly, yet my father would not let me go.　　3. I went to see the manager personally , for I had a very serious complaint to make.　　4. The bull rushed straight at the little boy, but he quickly moved to another side.　　5. I locked myself in my bedroom in order that I would not be disturbed by the children.　　6. We had waited for you for a long time, but you did not turn up at all.　　7. He was very pleased with himself as he had won first prize in the competition.　　8. The girl did not buy that expensive pair of shoes though she liked them very much.　　9. He walked out of the room very angrily and slammed the door hard.　　10. I shouted for help as loudly as I could, but no one heard me.　　11. You must come early so that we will have time to make all the arrangements.　　12. Neither I nor my brother stole the pears from your orchard. 13. I could not find him in his own house, so I went over to Alex's house to see if he was there.　　14. As we were walking to the other side of the island, we found a small stream.

English Grammar Juncture

英文文法階梯

康雅蘭 嚴雅貞　編著

專為想要重新學好文法的讀者所編寫的初級文法教材

- 一網打盡高中職各家版本英文課程所要求的文法基礎，為往後的英語學習打下良好基礎。

- 盡量以句型呈現文法，避免冗長解說，配上簡單易懂的例句，讓學習者在最短時間內掌握重點，建立整體架構。

- 除高中職學生外，也適合讓想要重新自修英文文法的讀者溫故知新之用。

Practical English Grammar

實用英文文法（完整版）

馬洵 劉紅英 郭立穎　編著
龔慧懿　編審

專為大專學生及在職人士學習英語所編寫的實用文法教材

- 涵蓋英文文法、詞彙分類、句子結構及常用句型。
- 凸顯實用英文文法，定義力求簡明扼要，以圖表條列方式歸納文法重點，概念一目了然。
- 搭配大量例句，情境兼具普遍與專業性，中文翻譯對照，方便自我進修學習。

實用英文文法實戰題本

馬洵 劉紅英　編著

- 完全依據《實用英文文法》出題，實際活用文法概念。
- 試題數量充足，題型涵蓋廣泛，內容符合不同程度讀者需求。
- 除每章的練習題外，另有九回綜合複習試題，加強學習效果。
- 搭配詳盡試題解析本，即時釐清文法學習要點。

Key Sentence Structures 100

關鍵句型100

郭慧敏　編著

● 介紹關鍵百大句型
整合歷屆大考曾出現的重要句型，於14個單元中說明
句型常在文章、段落中扮演的角色，讓您不需強記，
就能融會貫通，加以活用。

● 延伸關鍵百大句型
針對關鍵百大句型，再延伸、補充200個形似或同義
句型，讓您觸類旁通，事半功倍。

● 後附單元複習評量
除了有對應句型的練習題，每個單元後亦附評量，以
提供您即時練習、自我檢測的機會，讓您真正掌握句
型寫法，駕輕就熟。